PRAISE FOR *HOW YOU WERE BORN*

"*How You Were Born* is a stunning collection.
These stories are unsettling in the best possible way:
tender and pitiless, they take the reader by the hand,
by the chin, sometimes even by the throat. Look, they say,
this is what it is to be human. This is how strange,
how unspeakably beautiful, it can be."
—Alissa York, author of *Far Cry*

"Ghosts, tear gas, doppelgängers, child spies, a dragon
tattoo, midgets, weddings, mothers, and acrobats—Kate
Cayley probes the circus that is the human heart and
proves it to be wild and eccentric, big, and sometimes
aching, often bursting with wisdom. Every scene is vivid;
every character flesh and blood present. Every story in
How You Were Born is delicately crafted, full of drama,
epiphany, and strong emotion. Cayley's prose flashes
with insight—transparent and true. Here is new life."
—Lisa Moore

HOW YOU WERE BORN

STORIES

KATE CAYLEY

Book*hug Press
TORONTO 2024

FIRST BOOK*HUG PRESS EDITION

© 2014, 2024 by Kate Cayley
Foreword © 2024 by Alayna Munce

How You Were Born was originally published in 2014 by Pedlar Press

Library and Archives Canada Cataloguing in Publication

Title: How you were born : stories / Kate Cayley.
Names: Cayley, Kate, author.
Description: 10th anniversary edition.
Identifiers: Canadiana (print) 20230481620 | Canadiana (ebook) 20230481639
    ISBN 9781771668705 (softcover) | ISBN 9781771668682 (EPUB) |
    ISBN 9781771668729 (PDF)
Classification: LCC PS8605.A945 H69 2024 | DDC C813/.6—dc23

The production of this book was made possible through the generous assistance of the Canada Council for the Arts and the Ontario Arts Council. Book*hug Press also acknowledges the support of the Government of Canada through the Canada Book Fund and the Government of Ontario through the Ontario Book Publishing Tax Credit and the Ontario Book Fund.

Book*hug Press acknowledges that the land on which we operate is the traditional territory of many nations, including the Mississaugas of the Credit, the Anishnabeg, the Chippewa, the Haudenosaunee, and the Wendat peoples. We recognize the enduring presence of many diverse First Nations, Inuit, and Métis peoples and are grateful for the opportunity to meet, work, and learn on this territory.

For Lea

CONTENTS

FOREWORD

Like many good stories, my friendship with Kate Cayley began through a series of happenstances and affinities. I was the copy editor for her first book of poetry when we discovered we lived in the same Toronto neighbourhood and decided to meet at a local café to go over the notes I'd sent her. After we talked semicolons and line breaks and which-compounds-to-hyphenate for a while, our conversation turned personal. She and her partner Lea had two children who were conceived with the help of a friend acting as a donor, something I had just recently decided to attempt. A few weeks later I found myself at their kitchen table, talking cycle tracking with Lea, and I was moved by the atmosphere of easy, unsentimental hospitality and understated humour in their household.

A year or so later, I was newly pregnant when Beth Follett of Pedlar Press asked me to edit Kate's short story collection,

How You Were Born. And the first time I left my son with someone other than my mother for an evening was to attend the gala where Kate won the Trillium Award for the book. That was all ten years ago. Over the years, our families have become part of one another's lives through backyard parties, sleepovers, taco nights, teenagers babysitting younger kids, and so on—families formed in unfamiliar ways, doing familiar family stuff.

Kate and I regularly steal time away to have lunch or a drink—just the two of us. We talk books and politics and relationships. We talk about the struggle to make good art, and the struggle to be good. What I love about conversation with Kate is similar to what I love about her writing: she brings to the table a rare blend of intellectual curiosity and intellectual humility; a constant revising of thought away from received truths, toward nuance and fresh insight. I always leave Kate's company—and her stories—with a mind less certain than it was when I arrived, more open to the complications of the world as it actually is.

Recently, during one of these conversations, Kate described a blog post she'd read by Brandon Taylor on D. H. Lawrence and moral fiction, how Lawrence held that morality in fiction is "the trembling instability of the balance" and argued that "when the novelist puts his thumb in the scale, to pull down the balance to his own predilection, that is immorality." Rereading the stories in this collection ten years later, along with the three new ones, I'm struck by how assiduously Kate lets the balance tremble. In these pages, you'll find a world you recognize, even if part of you might not want to: a world in which even the seemingly well-adjusted are fundamentally adrift, misfits at heart; in which no moment of goodness or grace is untainted by some rejection or loss, some cowardice or self-deception, some profoundly unresolved underbelly; in which queer lives are not immune from moral shortcuts, ordinary awkwardnesses, and yes, familiar family stuff; a world rife with small moments of cruelty, clearly borne of pain; a world in which we long for, but can never have, "the splendid possibility of uncomplicated evil." These stories quietly (and with that same unsentimental hospitality I experienced in Kate's kitchen all those years ago) expose the pathos in our politeness, the mixed feelings roiling behind our composed exteriors, all the "unspoken knife-edges" in our daily lives.

One of my favourite passages in the book occurs near the end of the last story. Having just observed herself taking part in a silent, less-than-generous declaration of allegiance, the speaker addresses her imagined but as-yet unconceived child: "But you take sides. You have allegiances. You will discover that, when you are born. It's one of the first discoveries." Somehow, Kate Cayley lets her characters do what humans do, take sides, while never letting the stories themselves take sides, keeping them trembling in the balance.

You'd think a reader might feel dispirited by how starkly these stories reveal the way people happen to one another, the way we so often end up "wondering if anything could have been done differently." And yet you can't help but constantly catch the glint, tangled up in the moral haplessness of these characters, of a subtle thread of human beauty, perhaps all the brighter for being embedded in so much unvarnished truth-telling: we try to be good, we really do try.

I've always loved how, with the last story in this collection, we go back in time to before the first story; we travel from the ache of "There was so much they'd been too shy and decent to talk about, after all" back in time to "open-hearted and not knowing what to say." Maybe the trick of being a person (let alone a "good" person) lies partly in the effort of making that backwards journey again and again, from fixed to trembling. In daring the gamble, in spite of it all. These stories are a gift and a dare—a dare to look clearly at ourselves, and keep living.

Alayna Munce
Toronto

PREFACE

Writing is an odd business, mostly because it isn't a business. It is done out of love and folly, a mixture of grandiosity (thinking anyone ought to listen to your thoughts and imaginings) and self-abasement (unless you are a deluded narcissist you have to proceed on the assumption that you will work out your thoughts in a small space, alone, for a small audience, if you are lucky enough to have an audience at all). I don't mean there isn't a business to it: you have to be somewhat strategic, you have to juggle practicalities, you have to at least attempt to make some kind of living, one way or another. But you do need to persist out of love and folly, not practicality. And sometimes you get an unexpected gift.

In one of her autobiographies, Deborah Levy compares the experience of having a book go out of print to dying. I can't find the quotation. Perhaps she softens it by calling it "a kind of death." I don't know if the living can say much about what it is like to die, and I'm unsure about comparing a book, any book, to a person. But I know what she means. It does feel like something of yourself has left the world, some possibility of reaching a mysterious and unknown reader. When you write a book and have it published, you don't know who it will reach, or how, or what it will mean to them. When I started writing fiction, coming from the world of theatre, I was floored by the anonymity and intimacy. A theatre audience is by definition a group of people gathered together in a time and place. Whether or not a theatre performance "works" depends on the collective temperament of the audience in that particular time and place. With a book, you address a single reader directly, and they will encounter your work in times and places you will never know about. Even a few readers are enough for a book to have meaning. The book is a message in a bottle that you send out hopefully, but you can't predict who it will reach or how. The reader might not understand what you meant, or they might add something to your meaning, see something beyond what you saw. When a book goes out of print, that channel to a strange and unknown person, to whom you owe a debt, is closed down for good. Having a book rescued just as that is about to happen feels like a minor but significant miracle.

Short stories are sometimes viewed (maybe I'm being over-sensitive) as a secondary form, perhaps an apprentice form, a poor relation of the novel. Slight, resting in economy and avoidance, they are compressed worlds. A novel is a long haul, a journey. Alice Munro compares the short story to a house that you visit for a little while. You walk around inside it, look at the rooms, briefly experience what it would be like to live there, and then you go. That's what I love about them: they are modest in scope, they are fleeting. They seem like domestic spaces, restrained accumulations of small details that add up to more than the sum of their parts. As a reader, you can be shaken by how something so slight could contain so much. I could happily write them for the rest of my life. They have very few champions and not many readers. But they are interesting houses to step inside for a little while. I like to think a short story is a form with some humility in relation to the reader, who might read on the subway, while waiting to pick up a child from school, in the exhausted moments before bed. A story can sneak into your preoccupied life and will not take up too much of your time. A story can be a small yet quietly transformative thing, like an unexpected conversation with a stranger.

Having *How You Were Born* reissued has meant more than seeing the book rescued. I've also been able to rework some aspects of the original stories and added three new ones. I was pleased to find I still liked the book (there's nothing like the weird embarrassment of rereading past work, the sinking feeling that sometimes accompanies this), but I found it harder than I expected to add material that lived in the same world. In the intervening years, I'd become someone who wrote at more length, went on more digressions. The book, then and now, was meant to be short and pared back, to exist in a small sharp space. These new stories needed to fit with the older ones, as if they'd all grown at the same time, to share some of the same concerns: the terror and invisibility of both adolescence and age, the ambiguous responsibility we bear to our neighbours. While this was a challenge, I had a lot of help. And I was even able to resurrect a story that paired with the opening and closing stories of the collection, about two women and their daughter. This felt especially blessed. This story was built on a draft of one of the first stories I ever wrote, still in my twenties, with no children myself. I'd worked on it over the years, always reluctantly laying it aside. Now, finally, here it is, where it should be.

To be read, even by a few people, is to have witnesses. I think about this a lot. Everyone hopes, in some small way, to be witnessed. Most people have very few witnesses, and some people have almost none. The work they do is more or less entirely unrecognized. But to have your writing find readers is a particularly astonishing way of being witnessed. A piece of undeserved luck. When you read, you are a witness to someone else, to a world that is beyond your scope and yet is, for a short time, your home. You remain yourself and leave yourself at the same time. The reader and the writer recognize each other, even though they have nothing in common, even though they never meet.

But for that connection to happen, you get back to the business of writing, which is publishing: not the home the story is, but the home the story must find if it's to have any readers. Independent literary publishers are the champions of the short story, the poem, the novel that defies the accepted rules of narrative, the work in translation, the essays on politics and aesthetics, all things that might mean very much to the witnesses they have, but that will usually have very few witnesses. Independent presses are engaged in the business of writing, but they are also engaged in a work of love and folly. A small literary press is an enterprise of devotion, of hope, of belief in that reader, who will find the book and witness it. A small press is a business but also a gift. Having this story collection brought back into print, in a new edition and with new stories, is a gift. Like being invited back inside a house you thought was gone.

Kate Cayley
Toronto

RESEMBLANCE

There are three people in the car, driving to a house near Peterborough. The trees are beginning to turn, the grass stiffening with frost, the afternoon sky fading. The woman who drives is nervous on the highway. The other woman is profligate with her gestures, restless, drumming on her knees, rummaging through the bags at her feet, talking. In the back-seat their ten-year-old daughter listens to music, enclosed in a private world, looking out the window at the red and yellow leaves, the quick spatters of grey rain.

In the house, a woman is preparing dinner. She is alone; she is waiting. Her hair is grey with streaks of white, tied with a blue scarf, lopsided and too girlish. She wears jeans and a brown moth-eaten sweater. Sometimes she weeps without her face changing shape, keeps on working—this is common-place now. She doesn't cry around other people anymore. It's been eight months. Recently she even smiles, the side of her face catching the smile like a blow. There is clay under her short fingernails. Her clothes are clean but she is not. She smells very slightly, like wet newspaper, but no longer notices. Her son, Jake, who was forty, collapsed going into his apartment in another city far away. She has imagined his collapse over and over, a reluctant obsession. Did he feel the aneurysm coming but didn't know what it was? Headache? A clutch in his stomach? Was he afraid? Was there time to think? She imagines his body falling, herself in her house far away, not knowing. Imagines herself moving unknowing, the way she would imagine a stranger in a country that is about to be overtaken by disaster. That person spoke a language she has forgotten.

They stop at a gas station, Molly easing herself out from behind the wheel as if testing to make sure nothing is broken, Robin already outside, stretching, absently pulling a few leaves off the car. They both watch as Emma lopes through the sliding glass doors, heading for the bathroom, still wired into music.

The sun has come out. Everything is lifted, the shadows sharper, the trees darker. Mid-week, the highway is almost empty. Each car that passes hurls by them on the curve. How easy it would be to lose control, go too far to one side. That's all it takes, a forgivable lapse of focus, a small omission, and it's over.

"When we see her—" Robin swallows her thought, rubbing the fingers of her left hand with her right, shaking out pins and needles.

"What?" Molly says, too anxious today to be patient.

Robin scowls mildly at a point in the distance.

"What?"

"What should Emma call her?"

"Why should Emma call her anything?" Molly makes a face. Possessiveness or honest confusion, Robin can't tell which.

"But wouldn't it be kind?"

"It wouldn't be *true*." Molly is about to say something else that makes her seem less certain, less doctrinaire, but then Emma reappears. Robin kisses Emma's forehead, watching Molly, and Emma wrinkles her nose, wriggles away, butts her head against Robin's shoulder.

They never said *father*. They said *friend* to Emma at first, with a determined emphasis. Then they said *donor* but disliked the clinical connotation, like he'd given them a kidney rather than a drinking glass with half an inch of milky stuff at the bottom, handed round the bedroom door with a theatrical flourish. A daughter, growing, a serious baby, a serious girl, growing bigger now so that she often seems not to belong to any of them. Emma did not know him very well. When Molly and Robin stood together in the kitchen, crying (Molly still holding the phone in her hands), Emma stayed in the doorway, arms warily crossed.

"We have something to tell you," Robin said, surprised at how parentally calm she sounded, how grave. Molly tried to stop crying and hugged Emma, the phone digging into Emma's back.

"Jake passed away this morning," Robin said, touching Emma's hair, and then, not sure if Emma knew the expression, added, "Jake died."

Emma looked at both of them, and they could tell she was relieved, having expected a more immediate disaster, and that her sadness was mostly for them. It made sense that it wouldn't mean much to her, though they both knew that it would mean very much to her later, taking on the peculiar tug of something missing or unsolved. Knowing that, they left her alone.

They went to the zoo together, the four of them, the High Park Zoo where the animals live behind chain-link fences. Jake was visiting for a week, in the earlier years when seeing Emma had been a formal imperative, before they'd lapsed into distant goodwill. He walked beside Emma, asked her questions. She ran ahead to look at the emu, which had wicked red eyes and hissed, black-purple tongue darting out from the razor beak.

"If you put your hand through the fence," the zookeeper said, grinning, "this one will take your fingers off." He waggled his fingers and she laughed. Jake stood behind her, laughing too in that polite adult way. The older zookeeper looked suspiciously at his pierced ears, the tattoos on his arms, the leather cuff just above his hand on Emma's shoulder.

"You look just like your dad."

Emma laughed again. "No I don't!"

"Sure you do. You got his eyes."

She'd run back to Molly and Robin, repeating this joke. They'd said it was very funny.

Molly remembers Emma running, an unkempt little girl in dirty shoes with a flowered hair band sliding down over her forehead. She remembers Jake looking embarrassed and guilty, as if he wanted to ask for something or claim something he could never have. But he didn't ask, then or later, and maybe she'd imagined it. There was so much they'd been too shy and decent to talk about, after all.

Robin remembers Jake walking ahead, remembers an Orthodox family, bleached against their dark clothes, the mother following her five children, the father walking behind, talking into his cell. The mother was very beautiful, her face like marble, her whole body tensed toward her children as they climbed fences, shouting to each other and at the animals. Robin wondered about the woman's body under the lumpy clothes, wondered what the woman thought about her life, how she pictured herself in the eyes of others, or if vanity and longing were something Robin imagined for her, and this woman lived as a different creature. No, she thought, that's patronizing. There are no different creatures. But what if that was patronizing too—not to allow for how separate one life is from another. The husband, still talking into his phone, noticed Robin holding Molly's hand, frowned, and looked away. The eldest girl, maybe twelve, stared openly at a young woman standing next to her in a long black leather coat, her dark hair dyed blue like bird plumage. The children crowding at the fence reminded Robin of ungainly animals, their lives immeasurably foreign though (who knows) perhaps braver and more defiant than her own.

What Jake remembers is now closed.

The house is small. They're bunched in the hall, taking off wet coats. Elise insists on hanging the coats herself, while they shift positions and untangle sleeves, saying *please* and *thank you* too often. Emma, the centre of everything, is just young enough not to know it.

Elise didn't raise her children here; nothing in the house belongs to Jake except some boxes in the storage room that she is not sure what to do with. Books, mostly—the mystery novels he loved, literary theory he taught. Books with cracked spines, or not yet read, bought as a promise to himself for later, assuming uncountable days. It's a cabin really, one big room heated by a wood stove, a small bedroom added on, the storage room bolted shut, and an open pantry where a bulb with a paper shade lights up rows of jars.

A table made of reddish wood set with blue plates, mugs, a centrepiece of driftwood and leaves, anchors the big room.

Everything in the room is chosen carefully, carefully placed. The carved figures that line Elise's shelves, the pots hung from the rafters above the sink, the bowl of polished stones and beach glass on the coffee table, the quilt over the back of the couch. Elise is a potter; the plates and mugs and vases of dried grass and late-blooming flowers are hers. She sells her work at craft shows across the province, her signature glazes wild dark blue or a greyish blue that echoes the bluish tone of the clay itself.

"How was the drive?" Elise asks, then goes on without waiting, "I thought we could eat right away, it's all ready."

"We'd love to eat now," Robin says, thinking she doesn't know where to put her hands, that cutlery would give her something to hold. Molly keeps touching Emma and then catches herself and draws back. Emma looks around the room, goes to the fireplace. Elise rushes over and gives Emma a framed photograph from the mantle: Elise as a young woman, standing with her husband, son, and daughter in front of their house in Toronto. Everyone looks curious, beautiful, happy. Family myth-making, Molly thinks as she looks over Emma's shoulder, recalling the muddle and discontent and trouble of loving very young children. Though they probably *were* happy. Not as much as they seem to be in retrospect, but likely more than they felt they were at the time. Molly touches Robin's back and considers Elise in the photograph. They may be looking at Emma in twenty years.

Resemblances come and go—she looks like Molly, like Jake, even sometimes like Robin, known and unknown forebears showing up in her face.

The meal is fish, carrots and beans, biscuits, a salad, white wine, water in a glass pitcher. The flowers they brought seem inelegant next to the centrepiece. They spread blue cloth napkins on their laps, grateful that Emma talks freely and inconsequentially, looking from time to time at Molly to see if this is right. Elise is a relief too; she asks questions, smiles, the conversation skims along without too much awkwardness. They haven't seen her since the funeral, where she and her former husband had sat heavily, holding each other up.

Sometimes in the pauses Elise looks lost, sunken, but she recovers. As dinner goes on her friendliness becomes oppressive, as if she were speaking around a heavy object in her mouth, something cold or jagged, like metal. Choking, Molly thinks. Choked up.

As dessert (a pie made from Elise's own apples; she points out the twisted trees just visible from the window) is served (Elise briskly refusing help) and tasted and exclaimed over, Molly says quickly:

"We"—she almost puts out her hand to Robin, but thinks better of it, worried this makes Elise seem more alone—"we want you to know that if you want to see us—see Emma—in a more regular way, if that's something you want, we want that too. If you want."

A pause. Elise considers Molly, then leans forward, almost touching Emma's hand. Emma keeps her eyes on her food. This is promising, and Molly goes on more freely, tearing up.

"We loved him. We really loved him."

Elise leans back, picking up her fork. "I know. Thank you. It's not as if I didn't know." She adjusts the napkin in her lap.

But it's true, Robin thinks. They did love him. There's a framed photograph in their living room of the three of them before Emma was even a hesitant proposition. They're younger, swaggering drunk, ambitious, and, for that moment, iconic, lit up by the camera flash and the streetlight out front of the bar, as much a mythology as the family group, and as impenetrable.

"You know, I'm lucky in a horrible way," Elise says, after swallowing her mouthful of food. "He could've been my only one."

She stops abruptly, surprised. There's a fraction of confusion, and her face seems older. She looks around her like someone who's just walked into the wrong house. Then she smiles at Emma.

"But one is nice, too, of course."

Molly and Robin do the dishes, insisting until Elise finally waves her hands in front of her face in indulgent surrender. She refills their glasses, watching the three of them reflected in the dark window. Emma has gone to the couch with a book, picked from Elise's shelf without asking, and is reading, as she does anywhere. Robin is usually proud of this but now it seems rude, the casual entitlement of only children.

"Why don't we just see?" Elise says, answering the question in their minds. "Why don't we just see how we feel, later? I don't really know much right now."

Earlier, when they'd arrived at the house, Emma had stayed in the back seat of the car, wanting to hear the end of a song. Molly and Robin hadn't noticed. They'd turned at the front door, looking, calling, Elise already standing there, framed in the sharp spill of yellow indoor light. Emma tumbled out, slamming the car door and dashing up the short stone path, momentarily younger—a child afraid of being left. She'd come up short between them, gripping each by the arm, jostling for room on the top step, and Elise opened the door wide, inviting them in. Each of them, all three of them, saw the same thing, watching Emma run from the car. None of them say what they have seen, and it's not necessary to say. Jake's there, just for a second, fully there. Running toward them.

THE SUMMER
THE NEIGHBOURS
WERE NAZIS

My brother Richard was odd. By the time he was twelve my mother yearned for a diagnosis, but he was just odd. Oddness in a child is not tragic and doesn't gain you sympathy, but his strangeness felt to her as hard to bear and as isolating as real tragedy. He was afraid of the dark, afraid of strangers, cats, dogs, and other boys, and if anyone called him Rick he would say, "My name is Richard, please don't call me Rick" in a strained, grieved voice. He wore the same yellow T-shirt every day all through that summer. He would not eat bread crust. He thought we could send signals to aliens from our roof, given the right equipment. He became hysterical if my mother entered his room without knocking, and had a series of traps worked out so he would know if she'd gone in when he wasn't there. He was obsessed with the Third Reich and the nineteenth-century Society for Psychical Research, and he read books about them. He had no friends, except me, and wanted none. I adored him.

His teachers had no idea what to do with him, and he was hopeless in school. They'd say to my mother, "Well, his reading level is really just amazing…" and, drifting off, they would look at her helplessly, which made my mother, burdened with raising us on her own, lie awake at night thinking that a boy Richard's age shouldn't cry so shamelessly, or prefer the company of his nine-year-old sister, or be so content with his own solitary state. Richard prim-mannered, heavy-set, with chipped fingernails, stained clothes, and lank hair—barrelled through the world with implacable satisfaction, barely noticing his own social failings. Shoved against walls by students, mocked by bemused or possibly cruel teachers, he adjusted himself and continued, eager for the next discovery to recall at the dinner table, talking with his mouth full as my mother winced. Who could blame her—with fall came middle school, and she was sure it would kill him. She adopted a bantering, hectic tone with him all that summer. Richard, who missed nuance, noticed nothing.

That summer Richard decided we should spy on our neighbours, two old men who never left their house. He said they were Germans, high-ranking Nazi war criminals in hiding, and he stuck to his story even when my mother told him that Nazi war criminals hid out in Latin America or at least the BC interior, not Toronto. Besides, they were Polish, like everyone else on our street except us.

We made a lookout in the birch tree in our backyard. The tree grew against our fence, but the higher, thinner branches reached over to their side. If we edged our way out onto those branches, we could see, far below, their yard's thin grass and the cedar hedge they had grown to keep us, or anyone, out.

Calculated risk, Richard said to me, we are taking a calculated risk. He packed a bag for us to take up the tree. In it he put water, crackers, cheese, a flashlight, old heavy binoculars, a notebook and pens, and an air horn. I have no idea where he found the air horn. I put blue and white streamers in my pockets and hung them from the branches, against Richard's objections. I'm not sure whether he thought it made us too conspicuous or felt it introduced an incongruously jolly note to our mission, but he gave in when I begged.

"Nora."

"Yes."

"I need you to listen to me."

"Okay." I leaned forward, wedged in the branches, my stomach lurching when I looked down at the ground. He took out the air horn.

"Put your hand on the pin, there. That's what you pull to make the horn go off. Careful, it's really loud. This is only in case we have an emergency. A grave emergency. Pay attention, Nora."

Richard called the neighbours Friedrich and Wilhelm, pronouncing the names with a pedantically exaggerated German accent, like a villain in a movie. I called them The Men. We watched them through their one clear window. All the other windows were covered with newspaper.

The window looked into the kitchen. We could see an old white gas stove, a battered Formica table, a counter scattered with dirty dishes, cups with broken handles, bread ends. Sometimes the two men sat together at the table and drank coffee. Sometimes they argued, banging the table with their fists. Once one hurled a cup at the floor, where it smashed. After that they ignored each other for two days, moving quietly around the room, keeping their eyes down, not speaking, stepping over the white shards in their slippered feet. On the third morning the pieces had been swept into a corner, and the men sat again at the table, bent over their coffee and bread.

I wondered, and still wonder, which one of them swept up the broken pieces, coming downstairs in the night, shuffling into the kitchen, his hand searching for the light switch? The man who threw the cup, repenting, or the other man, forgiving? And why sweep the pieces into a corner, but leave them lying there? A reproach, or simply arthritic knees, acceptance of the inescapably encroaching chaos of poverty and age? Who were they to each other and what brought them to that house? Richard and I, so enthralled by the two war criminals in hiding, never considered anything nearer to the truth. Never-married brothers? Two widowers staving off loneliness and privation? Perhaps (though this is hard to imagine) old lovers, covering their windows in newspaper to hide? Or enemies, locked together in self-imposed isolation and struggle, malevolent in the limited light of the kitchen, the single naked bulb?

For us they were the splendid possibility of uncomplicated evil. It was Richard's ability to transform the world by the sheer force of his enthusiasm that made me willing to watch them for hours every day, to report excitedly on every movement, while Richard took notes. That was his gift. He would interpret every twitch, every mouthed word, and before my eyes they grew into sly architects of horror. It was an amazing gift: to give every observed gesture a secret meaning. His gift answered my longing for sense and significance in the world, just as I was getting old enough to begin considering whether any of us had much particular importance or place.

It might have seemed pathetic from the outside—the two of us, with our streamers and bag of supplies, shimmying up the tree after my mother left for work—but watching them was a duty and a calling. I don't know how we thought they wouldn't notice. Alone in their house day after day, they were as fundamentally unoccupied as we were. And for all I know, they speculated about us as much as we did about them. It never crossed our minds that we might be both the watchers and the watched.

The knock was loud. My mother answered in her bathrobe, clutching the Sunday paper. We were in the kitchen, watching her outlined in the doorway. We could hear her low voice and the man's shaky grumble cutting in and out. He was the slightly younger one, more hair, more teeth. She nodded, spoke, nodded, said something inaudible but final, shut the door, stood for a moment with her back to us. Through the window we saw him cut across our lawn toward his own house. He looked as though he were still mumbling, his left hand clenching and unclenching as he considered what my mother had said.

When she came back into the kitchen there were blotches of red on her cheeks, small isolated patches that made her look haggard. I was a child used to pleasing and hated to think I might ever be in the wrong. The whole time she spoke to us I stared at the red splotches on her cheeks, which seemed to be my fault. Wishing to be correct and praised, it never occurred to me that my mother might be an unhappy or easily humiliated woman. Not simply concerned with us, but in her own self: comfortless, at a loss.

She sat in front of us and announced in a brittle voice that we must stop climbing the tree. She wasn't angry, but we had to stop. She peered at Richard almost shyly. Richard looked out at the tree, hung with streamers now wet and tattered from summer rain.

"Richard," she said quietly, her voice less brittle now, "couldn't you *help* me sometimes?"

She waited while he stared out the window, his mind, as always, elsewhere.

She went upstairs, walking slowly to convey her disappointment. Richard smiled at me, picking at the hem of his dirty yellow shirt.

It was nothing she had said, so he missed it. He only noticed things said. I noticed. She was ashamed of him. I knew, though I didn't fully understand. Much later, having understood, it took me years to forgive her, and years after that to realize how unjust my grudging, high-handed forgiveness was. Seeing Richard as a sign of her bad luck might have been a necessary thing, a way of holding herself together, or attempting to. She didn't deserve to be forgiven as if I would, in her place, have behaved differently.

Richard said we must be more careful.

"There's still so much we don't know. We'll find everything out."

"Like what?" I asked, watching him rock back and forth. I felt doubtful, as if, for a moment, I saw him through my mother's eyes.

"Everything."

He waved his hands in the air.

"Everything, Nora. We'll find out everything."

I decided to believe him.

We went up the next morning, inching higher than we'd ever gone. The branches bent under us, the white curled bark slipping under our hands. Richard went first, testing with his weight, whispering for me to follow, the bag slung over my shoulder.

The two men sat in the kitchen. They did not seem to be speaking. The floor was piled with newspaper, spilling all around their feet. I handed Richard his notebook.

They must have been waiting for us. Chairs were pushed back, cups slammed down on the table, they moved with surprising force, opening the back door and running down the steps, one of them carrying a broom as if he would chivvy us out of the tree like stray cats. Richard watched, amazed. They stood under the tree, shouting in Polish. The one with the broom began to smack at the trunk. I thought that he would shake us down.

I pulled the pin on the air horn. The sound was so big I lost my breath. The men stopped yelling and stood open-mouthed, the broom held up in the air. Back doors opened all along our short street. People began calling to each other. Richard, startled, lost his hold and slipped down out of the tree, the leaves slapping against his face as he fell, down through the punishing branches and into the mud of a wet summer, but not wet enough, not soft enough. Richard stared up at me without seeing me, his leg twisted under him.

The air horn went on and on, taken over at last by a scream that came from my brother, strange and singular and out of place, as if coming from outside him, from the tree or the grass or the sky.

In the hospital (this was hours later, after neighbours, phone calls, paramedics), my mother sat with me in the waiting room. A doctor came out and said that everything would be fine, they were having some difficulty setting the leg, but everything would be fine. They would have to keep him sedated for a day or so but really, everything was fine. We should go home. We could come back tomorrow.

I slept in her bed. I think that was what she wanted. In the middle of the night I woke up and heard her crying in the bathroom, a stifled private sound that I never heard again and had only heard once before, listening with Richard after my mother was informed by my father, with a gentleness born of indifference, that what she'd told everyone was a trial separation was in fact permanent, something Richard and I (and probably everyone else) already assumed. Perhaps my mother, obstinately uncomprehending, was more like Richard than she knew. Lying in her bed, I longed for Richard's conviction that the world was organized and comprehensible, and took the sound of my mother trying to catch her breath as a sign that it wasn't and that she and I—and Richard too, though he didn't know it—were spinning in the dark.

Richard was fine. He said it had been a most interesting experience, and then he spent the rest of the summer reading, trussed up in a special rented bed. His leg had broken in three places. He limped slightly after that.

Years later, after the two old men had both died, the man who'd inherited the house wanted to sell it. Gentrifying neighbourhood, good-sized lot, good yard if you cut down the cedar hedge, late Victorian or at least you could pretend. With some work, likely a huge profit. The contractor who was hired by the inheriting nephew or cousin or whoever it was almost refused the job, every room stuffed nearly to the ceiling with newspapers, old mattresses, broken chairs. It looked, the contractor told my mother (Richard and I had both moved out by then, she was alone), like they had made some kind of intractable fort in there. Barricaded themselves in opposite ends of the house, each in his foxhole. Whatever secrets they'd kept, in the end they hid even from one another. Newspaper covered every window. And preserved in a corner of the kitchen, I imagine a broken coffee cup, and a broom.

STAIN

The day before the wedding, in the kitchen of the farmhouse, the groom, a man Mark had known since he was three and hardly ever saw, introduced Mark and Lena. They shook hands, Lena shifting the child on her hip. Before Mark could say anything she turned back to the stove and deftly placed her breast into the child's mouth, her loose shirt falling off one shoulder. Mark looked away, at his own face in the steam-blurred window. Through the steam he could just make out the mown lawn and line of bushes and the fields and the moon. The kitchen was full of the chatter of people he didn't know. He couldn't tell whether Lena remembered him.

Driving from Toronto through rural Ontario, he'd kept the windows of the rented car rolled up and the air conditioning on. The landscape made him uneasy. He'd read that the soil was soaked in chemicals, that farm animals ate compounds made from each other's bones. Even the fried egg sandwich at the roadside diner (*Come to Marcie's*, said the sign, blinking, half the bulbs burnt out) had stung faintly in his mouth, like bleach. The light was fading, and in the greenish-white glare of the headlights he strained to read the names on mailboxes, finding the house late and climbing out of the car dispirited, already wishing he had stayed home.

This was to be a confidently slapdash affair, held outdoors beneath a white tent that glowed in the nighttime garden. Mark stood on the patio, looking at the scattered people holding drinks. The couple's family and close friends had brought the food; most guests would sleep in smaller tents pitched in the far field. His own tent was rolled up in the trunk of his car. The groom, Brendan, had hugged him in a frenzied way and then disappeared. Mark had not yet met the bride. Brendan had pointed out his aunt, the wedding host, before hurrying off, and while Mark sipped his beer he watched Brendan's aunt and her wife, owners of the house and land (which they did not farm, he speculated, from the tidy look of them—perhaps they were lawyers or therapists or one of each). The two women were striding over the grass in rubber boots, surrounded by large panting dogs that bobbed and ducked around their legs. The moon hung low, yellow and soft and swollen.

A hand against his back made him jump.

"Sorry." Lena smiled, and the shadows on her face made her look gap-toothed. "I finally got Charlotte down on the couch. Thought I'd come and see you."

"How old is she?" He didn't know what else to say about the girl he'd seen in Lena's arms. He wouldn't have called her beautiful, even though he knew that was something people said when shown a child. Children, in idea and flesh, made him anxious.

"Twenty-three months adjusted age, she was born very early. I mean scary early." She grimaced briefly, looking down. "Isolette, blood transfusions, bone marrow transplant, whole nine yards. But we were lucky. It's why her forehead is so big, but she'll grow out of that."

She was smiling again, expecting him to smile in return. He imagined her in the hospital, looking into the plastic box that held, improbably, her tiny living baby.

"How do you know Brendan?"

He shrugged. "Old friends."

She waited for a question, then said, "Sophie's my sister." He looked blank. "Sophie! The cause of this disaster. I've been cooking since five this morning. I wish they'd just eloped."

A woman came out of the farmhouse through sliding doors. She looked like Lena, the same dark hair and sturdy fleshy body, slightly shining skin.

"Charlotte woke up," she said to Lena, who ran her hand along his arm, turned and went back into the house without looking at him. The glass doors closed softly.

At the Quebec City protest in 2001, Mark had been twenty-five, older than most of the other protesters with their emblematic shabbiness, their fierce sense of virtue. He'd been part of an Anglican delegation, which made him feel even older, worthy and temperate. He walked around by himself, clutching a camera, a witness and a tourist. He did not speak French. He felt surrounded by certainty and envied those who seemed to possess it. The people who threw tear gas canisters over the security fence, who started fires and smashed windows, who cursed the restaurant owners for locking their bathroom doors, and pissed anyway, in the street. Those who, without irony, thought of themselves as an army (they had that in common with the police). He hovered, envious, while also wondering if their conviction was anything more than a kind of primal and serious partying that singled out the cool and righteous. Not so different from a revival meeting, really, and with the same all-consuming spirit, the willingness to risk the body, to be laid open to confusion and harm—in this case, gas and volleys of rubber bullets and limbs broken out of sight of the cameras. He would not risk himself like that. He hung back, fiddling with the strap of the camera. He had read pamphlets and made signs and sensed an urgent if unspecific demand from the world that wanted answering, but he had no idea how to answer, except to come expectantly to a small stone city and march, yelling, through the streets.

On the first night, he met Lena by a bonfire at the base of a concrete column in an underpass. She was wearing a white dress and dancing in a crowd to music amplified by speakers set up in the open back of a van. She pulled him in, grinning. Sitting in the dirt later, they shared a bottle of red wine she'd produced from a backpack, and she spilled some down the front of her dress where it slowly darkened like old blood. She wore the same dress for four days, and each day of these four days she spent with him, as if that was what she'd intended to do, as if that was why he was there. Her face grew grey from sleeping on the floor and eating inadequate food. She leaned against him sometimes, but they never kissed.

He couldn't remember what they'd talked about, or even how much they had talked (everything was so noisy, probably there was not much talking). He did remember her stopping for a cigarette. She'd stretched out right on the ground and, looking up at him, squinting against the smoke, said, "The people. United. Will never be defeated," drawing out the chanted slogan. And then she giggled. A long extravagant giggle that grew and grew as if fed by doubt itself. She threw the cigarette away in a shower of sparks and stretched her arms over her head on the pavement, still giggling. Her friends were part of the Black Bloc, the ones who wanted to burn things and beat up cops, the ones who yearned for violence. So what was the giggle? Surely something had to matter? She offered her hand and he pulled her up.

He pitched his tent at the furthest edge of the field, where long grasses whisked against the nylon fabric. Trying hard to sleep, he was tormented by crickets and, unless he imagined it, a baby, wailing somewhere nearer the house.

Religion had faded out slowly. He stopped going to church, clearing room for a firmer, more assertive self, a self untroubled by faith or doubt, an invincible modern person, like the modern people living all around him. He'd hoped to jump into the land of that long giggle, that shower of sparks, that self-regarding unconcern. In the long run he had grieved; this regretless person had not emerged. The sense of loss had been gradual. He had a small apartment, which he dusted, and plants, which he watered. He had a clerical job in the office of an organization that raised funds for various beleaguered causes; he did not dislike his work. He had friends, and the face he saw in the mirror was friendly and attractive, even if he couldn't quite shake the look of desperation around the eyes. Rising late on Sophie and Brendan's wedding day, his head ached from the stuffiness inside the tent. He wanted coffee and felt a wave of apprehension, looking at the other, mostly empty tents and then at the house and the already teeming garden. Stacks of rented chairs were being unloaded from a van, plastic tables and a podium in dark wood, out of place in the bright morning. Trays of rented plates gleamed white. A group of women picked flowers for the tables, daisies and some pink flowers he didn't recognize. One of the women was Lena, with Charlotte wobbling beside her, pulling imitatively at blades of long grass and offering them to her mother, who exclaimed tenderly over each one. He could see how large the child's head was, how her neck quivered. Her shoulder blades stuck out like wings, her hair was wispy and scant, her knees a little bent. Fragile, barely saved. Lena looked hot and vivid in the sun. She waved to him.

"Mark! Come and help!"

Charlotte waved too, her skinny arms flapping up and down.

Walking alone in the upper city by the security fence, they'd turned a corner and had been enveloped in a cloud of tear gas, blooming white. Choking, they stumbled into a side alley, its silence broken by shouting and chanting from a few streets over, coming to them muffled, like a radio in an adjacent room. She looked up at him, her lids puffed and angry as if she'd been weeping for days, as if she were desperately unhappy. She leaned against someone's garage door, blinking back chemical tears, while he bathed her eyes with the saline they all carried. The intimacy of it had floored him.

"Let's get back."

"Where?" She was wiping her cheeks.

"Back to where everyone is."

"Don't want to miss it, do you?"

"Miss it?"

"Action! Action!" she growled, snaking her arm through his, holding the long skirt bunched up in her other hand, the wine stain faded to brown, like earth.

When they found the crowd she pulled him into the jumble of flailing arms, focused as a hive and pressing forward to the metal barrier, the row of police in riot gear facing them. She let go of his arm and fell back, and when he turned around she was gone, leaving him turning and turning in circles. He struggled through the crowd, tracing his way back to the empty street where the gas cloud overtook them, as if that might be a meeting place. There he found an old woman in a flowered housedress with faded seams, complaining to herself as she tried to scrub graffiti off her front door. The air was clear again, the sky brilliantly blue. Except for the graffiti it was an ordinary day, an ordinary street, and he was an unwanted stranger. He walked back to the underpass where they'd first met, which was still full of dancers and music. "This is a safe zone," a tall girl with acne traces across her cheeks said when he asked about a girl in a white dress. "We don't keep tabs on people."

He went home the next day, curling himself into a window seat on the chartered bus the church had hired, now full of exhausted congregants who either talked in high agitated voices or, like him, stared silently out the window at the farmers' fields. He finally slept, vulnerable as a child, his mouth open, eyes sore.

Coming alone to the wedding hadn't really been intentional, he'd just left it so long that there was no one to ask. But now he was glad of the empty seat beside him, pretending Lena might sit there, though she was with the bridal party, standing beside the podium in a tight sleeveless purple dress that made her look heavier, her breasts rounding in one mass, the skin on her arms mottled in brownish patches. Her dark hair was pulled severely back.

Charlotte sat calmly in the lap of a woman who had to be her grandmother. The woman kissed Charlotte's hair every few minutes and had a perplexed and pleased expression, her eyes open wide, as if the whole ceremony might be a joke. Mark wondered about Charlotte's father: who was he, where was he. He looked down at his slightly scuffed shoes. How often he'd thought about her. How little she must have thought of him.

How could anyone promise to *forsake all others*? Fidelity was one thing, but *forsake* made it sound like the couple entered a private wasteland. Surely nothing could justify a promise to reduce the charmed circle to only two. Cheers and shouts greeted the couple as they moved happily across the lawn. The chairs were stacked, the champagne popped. He was handed a drink and felt better. The sun beat down; the flaps of the large tent were rolled open; guests spread out over the grass. He worked his way toward Lena, who was standing with her mother and Charlotte. Lena smiled at him.

"Mark, this is my mother, Sylvia."

"Mark." Sylvia's voice was slow and hoarse. "Do I know Mark?"

"Mark is someone I haven't seen for a long time."

"Mark," she repeated, almost under her breath, holding Charlotte's wrist in one hand, the other tugging at a hank of grey hair. "Mark."

"Pleased to meet you." He took her hand, gently pulling it down from her hair. "Very pleased to meet you."

"Meet me?"

Then her face cleared; she remembered what to do.

"Pleased to meet you, Mark. This is a great day for me."

"You must be very proud."

"Oh yes."

She turned to Lena, who took Charlotte from her, prizing her fingers from the child's wrist.

"Why don't you get some food, Mama?"

"Food," Sylvia repeated, mimicking, "yes. Some food. Some food." She drifted away, pulling again at her hair.

"It's been five years. We're used to it now."

"I'm sorry."

"When Charlotte was born, she kept asking why I'd had a baby, why I'd done something so stupid. She thought I was a lot younger, I guess. Then she forgot totally and wanted to know why I was at the hospital all the time, was I sick?"

Charlotte struggled to get down, kicking at Lena's skirt. Lena set her on the grass, and she wandered off, pointing and smiling at people's plates, nodding her head. The groom laughed, forked food into her open mouth.

"Her dad stayed in Calgary," she said, as if he'd asked. "He works a lot. We have a house near a big park. It's nice.

He's a consultant for city planning. It's not oil money. Not directly anyway."

She clinked glasses with him.

"Cheers. To meeting up again."

She kicked her shoes off. They landed by a rose bush. She flexed up and down on her toes. Behind her in the crowd he saw Charlotte carrying half an orange.

"Nothing turns out like you expect, does it?" she asked. "You think you know how to live, how you should be living, you have all your ideas worked out, doesn't matter, you still find yourself—stuck. Just stuck. How it goes, I guess."

She grinned, as if to deflect what she'd said.

He pictured her in the house in Calgary, separated from the street by a green lawn, sunlight coming in through new windows onto polished wood floors. He pictured her playing in the park with Charlotte, lonely, beloved, fairly happy, the city rising round them in uncomplicated optimism, promising more.

"Where are you staying?"

"In a blue tent in the field."

She giggled, already slightly drunk, he thought.

"I'm in the brown tent near the house. But Charlotte's with me. She kicks."

He held his breath. She smiled.

Then the question had to come. "That day in Quebec City, why did you leave?"

She glanced away.

"That was a really long time ago."

He looked down, rebuked and ridiculous.

When he looked up she was running toward Charlotte and everyone else was falling back. Charlotte's arms were waving in the air, her face growing red, then purple, her mouth comically round and open, no sound coming out. The silence spread around Charlotte as more and more people saw Lena catch her up and reach into her mouth, saying over and over "out, out, get it out," but her voice was high and small and other louder voices said things like "call an ambulance" and "twenty minutes to get here, this far out," words blanketed by the sight of Charlotte going from purple to blue, her eyes bulging in her affronted frozen face.

Later, what Mark remembered best was Sylvia, standing next to her daughter, looking around at the faces of the guests, at her other daughter in her wedding dress, still holding her bouquet of pink and white flowers. Sylvia was saying something inaudible, and he wondered afterwards and for a long time what it was that she had to say in that moment when the unbelievable was happening—something that could not be, except that it was. In retrospect he felt he'd gotten a good look at the place where for the most part Sylvia lived, a place where nothing made sense and time opened over and over into something appalling and unreal.

He ran forward and grabbed Charlotte, stepping on Lena's dropped wine glass, which broke under his shoe. Lena let go and he took hold of the child, sticking his finger in her mouth and sweeping it across her plugged throat, again and again, until he felt something give and she spluttered and gasped and then cried. There was blood on his finger. His nail must have cut the inside of her throat. The cry grew into strong howling and Lena pulled her away without looking at him. She found a chair and tugged down the straps of her dress, both of her breasts out. Her breasts were swollen and veined. She kept her eyes shut tight, her face bent to the nursing baby, one hand held to her own throat. The fervour of the relief around him embarrassed him. He found his way to the kitchen, eventually joined by the farm's owners, who looked tired, joking that they were too old for this. Together the three of them washed and dried and stacked the supper dishes, while outside the party recovered and continued.

Around midnight he stepped out onto the deck. Guests were dancing, the bride swung round and round, shrieks of laughter as drinks slopped over. Sylvia had fallen asleep in a deck chair, just outside the circle of light from the kitchen windows. Lanterns flickered across the lawn. Someone had covered her with a shawl.

"Mark."

Lena was sitting on the steps holding Charlotte, who was asleep. She patted the spot next to her and he sat down. She didn't thank him, and he didn't want her to. Instead she kissed Charlotte's forehead.

"Sophie thinks I should wean her. But you know, she's not going to be small for long, she won't love me like this for long, I don't want to rush it."

He nodded. He thought about Charlotte in the incubator, in hospital, surrounded by the steady hum of machines, her body slight, reddish and translucent. The bulbous forehead, insect-thin arms, veiled eyes stung by the bright lamps. Tubes running through her, needles piercing her. Lena watching, anticipating loss, unable to believe in the reprieve even as the baby is put into her arms, finally able to look around, able to breathe on her own, to be brought into the world and her place in it, to be brought home. Look. This is sun, this is air, this is grass. Don't be afraid. I'm here.

Very slowly, he put one arm around Lena's shoulders, barely touching her. She leaned into him and sobbed so loudly he was sure someone would hear. This close, she smelled harsh and yeasty, the after-effect of her fear, and tears rose in his eyes. She'd remembered him only in passing, because of everything else that crowded him out, and now she would remember him as part of a great terror, another averted brush with disaster. After a while she stopped crying and he bent his face to the top of her head, letting his chin rest for a minute on her hair before she shifted a little and he, knowing he wasn't wanted, got up and went back inside the house.

BLOODY MARY

There was a small bathroom off of the gym's change room. Grace knew it was almost never used. It was behind a beige door between two rows of lockers, and it only had three cubicles. The bathroom was L-shaped, the cubicles facing the sinks and mirrors, and then a corner ending in a locked door. When Grace was younger, she and Eva had believed, or pretended to believe, that the locked door opened into a secret passageway, which led down and underneath the school. Now they both knew it was a storage closet.

Two years ago (when Grace and Eva were nine), the school had had an influx of cash and new bathrooms had been built for the gym, with windows and sensor hand dryers and posters in steel frames that advised taking a stance on bullying. But this bathroom had remained, lapsing into a glum afterlife. Fluorescents hummed overhead, yellowish-grey. The corridor to the storage closet was unlit, and Grace could remember when they had sat there on the floor, in the perpetual twilight, and pushed coins and small stones under the locked door, wondering what was on the other side of the shadowed line. Grace wasn't sure how long they'd done this for, or how long ago. She'd known Eva since preschool, which made it hard to figure out chronology. They lived two streets away from each other. They were only children. They took a circus arts class together and went to the same camp in the summer. Grace knew Eva's favourite foods, favourite books, what made Eva anxious, what she wanted. In university, when she was beginning to feel their hold on one another loosen, Grace read Emily Dickinson's "Where my Hands/are cut, Her/fingers will be/found inside" and wondered at the process of separation, how it had begun without her fully noticing, when for so much of her life she had been unable to think of herself without also thinking of Eva.

The three of them stared experimentally into the distorting mirrors—Eva on Grace's left and Avery on her right. Avery was new, to the school and to Grace. She was plump and wore a kilt and button-down shirt as though this was a private school, and Grace admired the costume, sensing it was a costume or disguise, like the red streaks in Avery's hair. Inviting Avery was Eva's idea, Eva who was trying to become a loud and daring person, on the lookout for new things and new people, like Avery. Grace understood she would need to be quicker, sharper, more dangerous, to keep up. She'd lined her eyes badly and put on a blackened metal choker of her mother's, which made a warm rash on her neck.

They'd played Bloody Mary before, once, at Eva's house during a sleepover, but nothing had happened. This second try was Grace's idea, though Eva had pounced on it, asking Avery along, bringing candles and a pack of Tarot cards, telling them that her mother had played something similar as a child in Kyoto, the game of Hanako-san, in which you must tap lightly three times on the third stall door in a third floor school bathroom and whisper *are you there* and a voice answers *here I am* and you push open the door to find a little girl in a red skirt who might drag you to the underworld. Eva's mother told her about Hanako-san because Eva told her mother about their plan to play Bloody Mary. Eva told her mother everything. These days, Grace told her mother nothing. She did not want to risk being interpreted. Evading her mother was a new but firm resolution, written in tiny script in the back of one of her notebooks. She couldn't tell if her mother had noticed yet.

Avery and Eva squatted down, rummaging through Eva's backpack. Cards, candles, incense, crumpled paper, a flattened plastic bottle, an oozing banana, crumbs, a brush clumped with hair. Grace shut her eyes: there was Eva's smell, and Avery's, stronger and unfamiliar and a bit sickening. Grace was very concerned with smells, since her own might suddenly overtake and undo her. Her mother lately wrinkled her nose, ordered Grace absently into the shower.

"Should I light the candles?" Eva asked, clutching them in one hand, the lighter in the other, flicking the lighter at Grace, who flinched.

"You afraid of fire?" Avery asked.

"No," Grace said.

They each held a candle into the flame, watched the wicks stutter and catch. Eva turned off the light and Avery jumped.

"Fuck off, don't do that."

Eva, giggling, turned the lights back on.

"This is so creepy."

They dripped wax in little pools beside the taps.

"Mine's not sticking," Avery said.

Grace took the candle from her, dripped more wax, held it carefully in the centre of the pool until it hardened. She hoped competence might make up for her shyness, her propriety, that she couldn't figure out how to say *fuck* without sounding self-conscious.

Eva reached for the switch.

"Can I turn the lights off for real now?"

She spoke to Avery, who looked at Grace, who nodded. The lights went out.

Grace and Eva's mothers were not friends, exactly, though they had become friendly over the years, because of their daughters, because they were both artists who were married to lawyers, because they inhabited a similar strata of middling artistic success bolstered by spousal affluence that meant they knew many of the same people. Later, Grace thought that Eva's mother had found her mother too literal, too chaotic, her chaos a form of aspiration; she was in fact fairly conventional, even the symbolic concerns of her paintings (sex, feminine childhood) skirting close to cliché, aiming for a wildness that had nothing to do with her actual life, her patient bombastic husband with his job in environmental law, her scheduled and enriched daughter, her hardwood floors and vacations. Or perhaps it was just Grace who thought that her mother was too conventional (this was when Grace was attempting to live in the woods with her girlfriend in a cabin with no toilet or running water, biking into the nearest town to salvage food from a dumpster behind the grocery store, an experiment that lasted until the first real snow). Grace loved the things Eva's mother made: miniature interiors full of perfect furniture, empty of human figures, as though everyone on earth had suddenly vanished. Dollhouses without dolls, Eva's mother called them, smiling from her stool, bent over her tools, wearing a headlamp. Grace would sometimes sit and watch her in her attic studio, while Eva, bored by her mother's work, sulked downstairs or played computer games with her father, both of them flushed and happy, yelling at the screen. Grace never asked Eva's mother what the arrangements of the rooms meant, suspecting she disliked the question. Grace imagined a sympathy moving between them as she sat quietly, watching Eva's mother create spaces that seemed more self-sustained than any place Grace had ever been in, free of history, free of people. Grace knew that the work was praised for the sense of unease it carried, but to her there was nothing safer than those empty rooms. She was old enough to realize that the peace she felt stemmed from Eva's mother leaving her completely alone, not old enough to understand that was because Grace was not her child.

Grace was her mother's subject. In another era, she would have been called her mother's muse. She appeared in almost all the paintings, wearing petticoats, seated on strangely carved thrones, outlined in light from an obscure source, something about her face or body subtly altered. Sometimes her mother incorporated photographs, though with the face scratched out. Her first solo show had been a series about pregnancy in which a woman appeared to carry not a baby but an ornate tumorous growth, sprouting extra eyeballs and tufts of coarse hair. Grace had found an interview archived online in which her mother talked about the fear of the unborn baby, how it was linked to the fear of death, that other future that the body carried. Something eating you inside. She was pregnant herself, with Grace, and in the photo above the article she glowed with health, beautifully curved, in a long dress, hair like honey falling from a spoon, humming with life, as though she would interrogate death but never actually die.

Grace still appeared in her mother's work, but seemed to be frozen around age eight, her present self too knobby and intractable. The more recent paintings had not been well received by the sole critic for an online art magazine who had noticed them ("exploitative kitsch") and her mother had cried on and off for days, sometimes in bed, sometimes feeling her way around the house. Grace, who did not think of herself as cruel, had been privately pleased, her mistrust of her mother vindicated. Grace was growing prudish and severe, and would remain that way for a while, but it was a necessary step to developing a sense of decency.

When Grace was much younger, her mother took her to the library after school. They came out together, lugging books; she was looking up at her mother when her mother shot her arm in front of Grace as though stopping her at the edge of a cliff. There was a man lying in the road, a car stopped in front of him and a woman getting out of it, all the cars stopped, a little ring of people gathering around the man, but Grace could see over their heads from the top of the steps. No one seemed to know what to do, even the people who were on their phones calling for help hoping someone else would take over, and the people not holding phones flapped their hands uselessly, not sure if they should touch the man. The woman who'd gotten out of the car bent over him. She was young, young enough that Grace could imagine being her, would have wanted to be her if she'd seen her somewhere else. She was wearing a white sundress printed with huge pink roses.

"I'm sorry, I'm so sorry, are you okay?"

She was trembling.

"Are you okay, are you okay?"

The man began to howl, a keening sound that had no relationship to language, and as the howl grew louder his shirt grew red, soaking red, and it seemed to Grace that the sound he made was calling the blood out of him slowly, then faster.

"Oh God," the woman said. "Jesus, Jesus, Jesus."

Grace's mother dragged her back into the library and held her on her lap, explained that the man would be fine, and Grace made a convulsive movement in her arms, suspecting a lie. When they went back outside at last, the man and the woman were gone, though the car was still there with the door open and the road was closed, a line of police tape around the red stain. The stain, beginning to dry, had a wobbling outline, the drops spattered around it islands off the coast of an unknown country. Grace heard her mother gasp the way she did when the world astonished her, even as she covered Grace's eyes with her hand and led her gently down the stairs. And there it was, in her next painting, the exact red shape; her mother must have taken a picture on her phone as she shielded Grace. Later, when she was attempting to create a story about her mother for herself, she thought of that as one of the first clues that her mother could not be trusted. She could eat anything up, anything at all, and would not think twice about it.

Around the same time, Grace began to have dreams in which someone was shovelling earth into her mouth, gritty mouthfuls that spilled out over her lips. She could not swallow so she choked but because it was a dream she kept on choking, spluttering and choking, as if her gullet could always be crammed fuller. Hard gobs at the back of her throat. She knew someone was feeding her, she could infer intention, an arm, thin as a spider, grasping the handle of the spade, stuffing her face with a regular motion that combined mechanism and ill will. As she spluttered and protested, she had the sense that there was a voice somewhere at the end of the arm and that the voice was about to speak to her.

"Is it like being buried alive?" her mother asked (Grace was still telling her mother things then).

"No," Grace said. "It's like someone feeding me dirt with a shovel, or maybe a spoon."

"Being buried alive is a very common dream," her mother said encouragingly.

"But I'm *not*."

"It means a lack of control. Being buried alive. Or loose teeth, too. Do you feel a lack of control?"

"No," Grace said.

In her mid-twenties, she'd described the dream to a therapist after her mother died, and the therapist had suggested that the person attached to the arm, the voice she expected to hear, was her mother's, which made Grace want to laugh and made her decide against therapy. It reminded her of her mother, someone naively prodding her toward a conclusion, sure they knew what everything meant, or that understanding meaning would lead to something solidly attainable, a virtuous brilliance that would illuminate her life. When she thought about the dream, which still disturbed her even though she no longer had it, she wished she was not doubtful about repressed memory, wished she could believe that the dream was telling her something real, something she could recover knowledge of, work on, work through. It might have reassured her, diffused some of the dream's power, the physical shudder of the dirt in her mouth. She would have preferred—no, not preferred—would have in some way been steadied by the thought that the dream, or her mother, if examined carefully enough, might reveal a single truth. But she didn't have enough faith in interpretation. Things like the dream just bubbled up from somewhere, unexplained and unexplainable, and you had to look at these things squarely sometimes but not too much, not too often, because you just had to live. You lived with things that could not be made meaningful in the same way you lived with the shape of your nose.

With the lights out, their three faces swam into view in the mirror, and the flames made them look solemn and melancholy, each one admiring herself, Avery dragging her hands through her hair and shaking it around her face.

"Close your eyes," Grace said.

Avery and Eva shut their eyes, Eva squeezing hers tight as she always had, like a toddler faking sleep. Avery's lids trembled, and Grace, who had kept her eyes open, thought she could see her looking. Grace, to make the moment more serious and to feel she was piloting the situation as she should, took Avery and Eva's hands in hers and squeezed. Eva's small hand squeezed back, Avery's limp, her palm warm and a little damp. Grace could see her smiling in the mirror, as if she was making fun of her, making fun of the game, as if she had something Grace wanted that she would not give her. Grace hoped to impress her and didn't know how.

"Bloody Mary," Grace whispered.

It was Eva who'd first talked to Avery, her friendliness toward a stranger later becoming fascination. Eva was friendly. It was Grace who calculated social advantage, who didn't risk herself. Eva and Grace were both sheltered and untested and were beginning to yearn for what seemed hazardous, at least by proxy. Avery walked herself home at dusk or was picked up by her mother's boyfriend, who waited by the schoolyard fence, something in his stance catching the attention of Grace's prudent father (also there to pick up his daughter), the way that men sense the possibility of violence in each other without saying so, so it manifests only as disdain. Grace's father looked over and looked away, his hand on Grace's shoulder. She shook him off.

Eva trailed after Avery, and Grace, as Avery's hand tightened and hurt her, understood the lure of her.

"Bloody Mary," Grace said.

Avery frowned and Grace wanted to know why and wanted Avery to concentrate and she let her hand drop, and Avery, not meaning to or maybe meaning to, ran her finger lightly along Grace's palm.

Later on, when Grace thinks of Avery and what she con-jectured of Avery's life, she feels shame. She is drawn to people (as friends, lovers, causes) who seem more wounded than she feels herself to be. She is intrigued and energized by concealed or displayed hints of brokenness. Once, at twenty-one, she passed by a young woman smoking in front of the dive bar near the other more self-conscious dive bar where she worked on Saturdays (this was itself an affecta-tion, her parents gave her all the money she could want), the woman fraught, pulling on the cigarette, laughing into the face of the man standing beside her. She was a little older than Grace and looked like she'd lived hard already—and might live harder. Grace saw, tattooed in clear capitals along the woman's neck, NO ONE CAN SAVE YOU, but the words had the opposite effect on Grace: she wanted the woman, and she wanted to save her. She had wanted to save Avery, and it shames her later, when she tries to stop herself from thinking she can save people, because it is patronizing and self-serving and it makes her unhappy. Grace wants some peace in her life now, she wants to live alone, she wants to build tiny rooms and fill them with tiny furniture but no people, Grace is still given to extremes.

"Bloody Mary," Grace said.

Avery opened her eyes.

"There's someone in the mirror," Avery said, her voice so soft it was almost only breath.

"No, no, no, I don't want to look," Eva said.

"She's looking at you, Eva," Avery said.

Avery turned to Grace and winked, then reached over and lifted a strand of Grace's hair and brushed it along Eva's cheek and Eva screamed and opened her eyes and flung herself away from the mirror, knocking one of the candles into the sink.

Grace knew Eva's fear was real; she recognized the way she threw herself backwards and the timbre of the scream and the candle guttered in the sink. Eva, tangled up in her skirt (she'd worn a long skirt, lacey along the edge), crawled away from the mirror into the dead end of the L-shaped space. Grace could see her legs sticking out.

When her mother died, Grace sat with the body in a room in the palliative care ward. Her father had gone to get them both some food. The death was a long time coming, and both Grace and her father knew the staff well, knew the places where the floor dipped, the toilet in the bathroom that didn't flush. Her mother's body was excavated: breasts gone, ovaries gone. Grace had given her mother a wig made of human hair, golden as Rapunzel's, which cascaded over her sharp shoulders, bright on the faded blue of the hospital gown. Her mother, skeletal and rarely speaking, had allowed Grace to fit the wig over her scalp, had smiled into the hand mirror with such tenderness and gratitude, and Grace had been sorry, for her secretiveness, for the way she'd left home, for her feeling, right up until that moment, that she would not keep her mother's paintings or talk about her with friends, that she would let her be entirely dead. Now, as they both grinned conspiratorially into the mirror while her father looked away (he hated that wig, he thought it was monstrous), Grace felt with relief and panic that she had been wrong, that she would talk about her, constantly, obsessively, that she would even pardon her mother for thinking that Grace was hers to repurpose, to keep.

Standing over her mother's body, Grace gently loosened the wig and put it on her own head (her hair was very short). In the hospital room's private bathroom, she looked at herself in the mirror, a vision of the kind of young woman her mother had wanted Grace to be. She shut her eyes. Googling idly one night while her mother had slept in the hospital bed, she'd read that one theory about the success of Bloody Mary games was that it involved something called dissociative identity effect, meaning that if you stared at yourself hard enough and long enough you would cease to recognize your own face, and she thought of her mother, staring at Grace until Grace became someone else. She tried it now, opening her eyes and glaring at herself under the wig, her skin greenish with exhaustion and grief, but no other face appeared. Just herself, in all her terror.

After she'd sent her father home to see if he could sleep, she phoned Eva, who Grace didn't see that much anymore, Eva who lived with a man Grace didn't like, and Eva left the people she was with and took a bus across the city and swept down on Grace out of the night, the only person she wanted near her, Eva with her hair wet because she always forgot to bring an umbrella, and Grace threw away the cigarette she wasn't smoking and Eva held her and she howled, a huge sound like the man hit by the car. Eva didn't say anything, rocking her under the orange streetlight.

Grace switched on the bathroom lights. Eva was half-lying, half-sitting, her legs drawn up now to her chin, shivering.

"There's nothing there," Grace said. Avery snorted behind her, blowing out the candles. Grace crouched beside Eva, squaring her back at Avery. Grace put her hands on Eva's shoulders and shook her, like she used to do when they fought, pulling Eva back, it's nothing, there's nothing there, I promise, I won't ask you what frightens you or why, I will just be here, I am here, I won't persuade you of anything, you don't need to be afraid.

"It's just a game," she said.

MIDWAY MIDGETS
AND GIANTS,
PHOTOGRAPH 1914

The big ones held the small up to the light. War was not much of a disruption for them. No ordinary life was ever promised.

In the picture, most of the faces are serious, self-important, in keeping with the camera's role as sombre chronicler. They are used to being photographed for the local paper of every town, sometimes posing beside an admiring farmer who off-sets the spectacle of huge or tiny limbs. They know the drill. Stand in a line arranged by height. Behind, tufts of dead grass and the gaping tent flap, stained and fetid as a diaper, opening into darkness. Stolid eyes. But a few of them are caught in a grin, blurring the print, a rupture in the frame.

October 1914, and the fall fair shows are upon them. Dogged and quarrelsome, they grind their way across Ontario by train. Boredom reigns. They have seen these towns before and the towns have seen them. The murmur in the air now is for war, and they are useless as soldiers or nurses. People come, but their attention is elsewhere.

Rose Dalrymple, "Little Rosebud," two feet seven inches, sneers at the camera, blonde, beribboned, bird-boned, perched on the shoulders of the Giant Joseph, eight foot five. She feels the fine dust left by a hot summer blowing into her eyes.

"Put me down, Joe," she mutters, "my fucking legs are asleep."

And he does, as soon as the photographer turns away, sliding his hands across her breasts, grunting laughter as she spits, but not far enough.

When Tom Thumb (two foot one) married Lavinia Warren (two foot three) in 1863 in New York City, two thousand people attended the ceremony. The train of her wedding dress swept along the marble aisle of Grace Episcopal Church. Her hair was pinned around her waxy, happy face. P. T. Barnum, whose circus they performed in, sold five thousand tickets to the reception. The newlyweds rode in a tiny silver carriage through New York streets thronged with cheering crowds. Her white-gloved hand waved from the open window. His hand lay protectively on her knee. Afterwards, drinks with Abraham Lincoln and a honeymoon in Europe.

Rose has seen the wedding photographs. At night she lies in her berth on the rocking train and thinks about Tom Thumb and Lavinia. She draws her hands down her body. Seventeen. At the bottom of her trunk, a wedding dress, wrapped in newspaper to keep off the dirt that settles through her clothes.

She is pretty, and this makes her valuable. Every night when people pass through the tent to hear an instructive lecture on "Curiosities and Marvels of the World," she is given pride of place. She steps forward, smiling, twirls, sings a song in a quavering sweet voice. "Little darling," the orator coos. "Look at her. Pure as the child she'll always be." He kissed her once, late one night when she'd gone into the field for a piss, so drunk he was nearly ass over teakettle, the only man who has taken that liberty. She hates him for it.

She sits on the grass to eat her lunch, a slab of meat between two slabs of bread. The cook is German and is lying low these days. Rose does not dislike her but is not going to talk to her either. Positions are so unstable.

On the honeymoon tour, Tom Thumb and Lavinia stayed at the finest hotels, and crowds followed them wherever they went. Gracious, smiling, they waved and waved, retiring at last to the sanctuary of their room. Honeymoon over, they came home to a Manhattan mansion, a sloped green lawn, a yacht, a private car on train journeys. The couple, among the most famous in the world, walked arm in arm in their garden.

Joseph sits with her, though not close. She pouts over her bread. He munches very slowly, looking at the sky.

"Good weather," he says at last.

"That's so."

"Port Hope tomorrow, that's a good crowd."

"I don't care if it is."

She kicks at the dust, digs trenches with her high-heeled boots. The manager dislikes these boots for the height they add.

Joseph looks at her, puzzled. She tears up a handful of grass and throws it at him.

"What's that for?"

He is so easily hurt. It's like crumpling a piece of paper.

"Are you mad at me from before? It was only a joke."

She thinks, but is not sure, that she could make him cry if she wanted.

"Only a joke," he repeats, shaking his head.

"Come here."

And he heaves over and is happy. That is easy too.

They sit and eat, not speaking. Tonight, she thinks, she will see in the audience a man in a grey suit, black patent leather shoes, straining on tiptoe to see her, for he is as small as herself. But not like her, jostled, sooty, shunted from town to town. A small man from a big circus in New York or Chicago or even less glamorous—Philadelphia or Denver, just somewhere that is not here. She will be whisked away to wider skies and top billing and will take with her only the wedding dress. It is white silk, given to her by the aunt in Kingston who sent her on the road, the aunt who taught her to sew invisible stitches, who pricked the needle into her wrist if she was lazy. The dress is trimmed with blue ribbon and lace torn from discarded costumes. She parades in it before the distorting mirrors, late at night, alone in the tent.

"I will go away, Joe," she says now, "you know that?"

He shakes his head.

"I will go away to be married."

"What about me?"

She touches his hand, brushing her fingers along each knuckle.

Then she gets up and skips off. Bright-faced, gleefully cruel.

When Tom Thumb died of a heart attack at forty-five, he was one of the richest men in America. Astute, personable, he showed a lacquered benevolence to the world, and the world loved him. He was buried under a life-sized statue of himself. At the funeral, weeping into a black-edged handkerchief, Lavinia walked veiled behind his coffin and the mourners who lined the New York sidewalks felt lumps rise in their throats.

Rose has the photograph of Lavinia at the grave. It is wrapped up inside the dress. Perfection and a beautiful end.

That night, she steps forward on cue, sings her song while scanning the crowd for the face of her husband. The crowd is patchy and indifferent. It's easy to see there is no potential husband watching her. It doesn't matter, she thinks, stepping back out of the light. Another night, another place.

She is young and still has time. In the perfunctory applause, she curtsies, fluttering her eyelashes, which are stiff with dots of blackened wax, blowing kisses from her shiny, painted mouth.

Afterwards she ducks out the back of the tent.

"Cigarette?" asks a voice from the shadows. She knows who's there, because this is their game, every night this is their game, and the shadows resolve into Joseph and he holds the cigarette package over her head and she leaps for it, making him laugh, and he holds it up out of her reach and she jumps again, barking like a trick dog, laughing too, and suddenly they are both happy, and even if the happiness is flimsy and humiliating she doesn't care. Her skirts fly up above her waist and he watches her, she kicks up her skirts on purpose, the lace frothing up into her face. And his eyes are wet as he tosses her a cigarette and takes one himself, he leans in and lights hers, and they are quiet, pulling on the smoke, watching it waft away into the dark.

HEIRLOOM

Emma stood on a bench in the backyard, reached for the winking red stones. I couldn't remember the old woman's name. She wore a dark red velvet dress, the hem dragging on the grass, and a belt made of brass links, cinched at her waist, her grey hair drawn tightly back with combs. She was out of place among the younger couples, in their expensive jeans, sundresses. Emma reached for the earrings again.

"Look, Mama."

"Careful, Emma."

"Oh, they're only costume," the woman said, straightening up. She looked around. "Have you seen Roger?"

"I don't know," I said.

I didn't know who anyone was. My partner was talking with a group of men I'd never seen before. Lydia, the hostess, had greeted me warmly and run off and was now setting down platters of food, calling instructions to her husband. I paid exaggerated attention to Emma and wished I'd worn a different dress (the wilted green cotton checks now reminded me of a tablecloth), until the woman, drawn by Emma, came over and spoke to me.

A man, older than me and younger than the woman, appeared and took her arm.

"Oh, there you are, Dorothy."

"Yes, dear."

He held out his hand.

"I'm Roger."

"Molly."

"And who is this wonderful person?"

"This is Emma. My wife is over there," I said, waving to Robin, who didn't notice, but I calculated that Roger would have a small surge of fellow-feeling, perhaps tempered with the wistful bemusement of his generation at my inherited good fortune in having a daughter, or a wife.

"How old is Emma?" Roger asked.

"She's five."

And then, with nothing else to say, we admired the party and the neighbourhood; he asked me when we had moved here, and that got us to renovations, the shocking price of houses, the fate of new immigrants and the working poor in the city's competitive market, Roger and I genuflecting to our obscene luck, hoping it would hold, while Dorothy looked confused. He asked me if Emma would start at the nearby school in two weeks and told me he taught there himself, as Dorothy had before she retired.

"When did you retire?" I asked her.

She considered.

"Oh, twenty years ago, at least. Yes, I think twenty years."

We waited.

"It was a rough school. When I started. Oh yes, it was."

We waited again, Roger with a cheerful apprehensive expression, like Robin when Emma was learning to walk.

"Should I escort you home, Dorothy?"

"Oh yes. Thank you."

She shook my hand.

"Goodbye, darling," she said to Emma, who wiped her mouth on the red dress.

"Emma! No!"

"It's all right," Dorothy said, smiling. Then she unhooked her earrings and held them out.

"Oh no," I said. "No, no."

"They're just costume, not valuable."

"Her ears aren't pierced," I said.

"Yours are," Emma said.

Dorothy held the earrings out to me, and when I blushed and shook my head, she placed them in my palm, closing my fingers. Emma clasped her hands in agonized delight.

"Thank you," I said.

She took Roger's arm, and he led her out the side gate. I had no idea where either of them lived.

"Do you think she means for you to keep them?" Robin asked on the way home.

"It's not appropriate. I'll return them."

"How?"

"I don't know. I'll ask Lydia where she lives."

"You should put them away for Emma. You know, as an heirloom."

"They aren't valuable."

"That's not the point of an heirloom. Do you think she knows he's queer?"

"Who?"

"Dorothy. He takes care of her, Omar said."

"Who's Omar?"

"Lydia's husband. I like him. He's a musician. I think Saul is going to be in Emma's class."

We passed the school, pointed it out to Emma, as we did every time we passed. She ran ahead without looking, jumping back obediently at the corner.

"Of course she knows. She's old, not an idiot."

We took Emma's hands. Robin leaned over and kissed my neck just below my ear.

"Just think of the earrings as a sign we're supposed to be living here."

We paused before going into our house, looking up together at the upper windows, ritualizing incredulous satisfaction at our ownership. Marriage, child, house, neighbours, school. Parent council, meetings with teachers, petitions delivered to our city councillor. Loyalties, minor disagreements that seemed significant at the time. I didn't mind. That was what the future was supposed to be. That was the future that anyone would hope for.

We had moved three months earlier, in a flurry of optimistic panic and parental help with the down payment. Robin finished her PhD (sexuality and fantasy in children's literature) after ten years of intermittent focus. I got a part-time job as a children's book editor. Emma turned five. I made plans: painting the kitchen blue, tearing up the pink marbled linoleum, pulling the green plastic runner off the stairs. Robin took Emma to the park. I tugged and coughed, became friendly with the man at the hardware store who gave me advice, filled contractor-grade garbage bags with the past lives of strangers, who I thought of as spirits of the house. On a shelf in one of the closets I found a diorama of Leonardo's Last Supper, with a little bulb behind to illuminate the sticky plastic faces. Robin would have laughed at it, perhaps insisted on keeping it as a kitschy artifact of the previous owner, but I threw it away. When a letter arrived with a return address in Portugal, I threw it away too. The house was now mine.

I examined the earrings in the bathroom mirror while Robin got Emma into her pajamas. I set them on the windowsill, thinking I should find a box, put them away. For Emma, for later. I had a drawer where I put things like that. Things I hoped she would want to keep, take with her when she left me. I looked at them again on the windowsill, sitting beside a roll of toilet paper, a half-empty bottle of organic shampoo. I could hear Emma and Robin upstairs, pretending to be bears, rumbling under the covers.

The house was almost finished now. The kitchen painted, the cancerous broadloom thrown away, the brick exposed. Even with the unpacked boxes still stacked in the corners, we had settled.

"Come up!" Robin called out, her voice muffled, "we're ready!"

In September, Robin went back to sessional teaching. Emma started school. I ran into Roger at the head of my street and asked him if I should go see Dorothy and give her back the earrings.

"Oh no. It would upset her."

"Would she think it was rude?"

"She won't remember giving them to you."

"You're very good to her," I said.

He raised his eyebrows. "I've known her for a long time."

Instead of saying goodbye I invited him for coffee, and he came. It was a Saturday, Robin had taken Emma to buy new shoes, texting me pictures of pink runners, preposterous bows. Roger followed me down the sidewalk and didn't offer to help with the groceries I was carrying. When we got inside he examined my bookshelves while I put the food away, talking brightly.

"I am going to buy a farm," he said, turning to face me, hands in his pockets.

"Oh," I said.

"I just had a meeting with my real estate agent, looking over properties. I don't want something that needs a lot of work."

"This place needed a lot of work."

"I'm too old for it. I want something ready to go. Near a town. With some woods to walk in. A fireplace *and* a woodstove. I'm greedy, I want both! And near enough to the city."

"Would you commute?" I asked.

"Oh goodness no, imagine! No, I'll be fifty-five next year. I'm taking early retirement."

"Will you miss teaching?"

He seemed taken aback for a moment.

"No," he said slowly, "no, I won't. I've wanted this for a long time. I'll sell my house. I'll grow vegetables, I'll have parties for friends. A few guest rooms. I'll read. I'm tired of Toronto. I'm tired."

He pulled out his phone, showed me listings. I admired the listings, glad to have something to talk about, glad that I could now make friends with him without second-guessing his fussiness, his deliberations. It was finite; he was leaving.

We sat and drank coffee. We found we liked similar books.

"I'm sorry you'll be going," I said, when he got up. "It would be nice if you could teach Emma."

"I don't know what I'll do about Dorothy," he said, lacing his shoes.

"She will miss you," I said.

"I care for her," he said, "and she's been very good to me."

"We had a Michael Jackson conference today," Emma told me when I picked her up on Monday. She wore pajamas and her new shoes, burgundy runners with blue ribbon laces. There was gum in her hair. I wished Robin would stop packing it in her lunch. The wind was turning cold.

"Do you mean a concert?" I asked encouragingly. "A Michael Jackson concert?"

"No. It was a conference. We ate waffles and Froot Loops. There were parrots."

"Who gave you the waffles and Froot Loops?"

"Not for real."

"Who else was at the conference?"

"Mitchell and Miles and Sadie and Quinn. Then Mitchell threw up. Sadie stepped in it. Tonya washed her shoes."

The wind was cold. Some of the children wept by the wall.

Roger sometimes dropped by on Sundays, when Robin went with Emma to see her parents. I liked Robin's parents, but we'd gotten into the habit of Robin taking Emma away on Sundays when I had been home with her all the time, and now we kept it up even though I was often alone in the house.

He brought squat tarts from the Brazilian bakery, complained about the new coffee shops with their vegan cupcakes.

There were more photographs, offered across the table, tiny on his phone screen, though once or twice, when there was some detail he really wanted me to notice, he would pull out a laptop, make me shift my chair. He traced lines above the images with one finger, speculating on the life he imagined, told me about what he called the balance between *prospect* and *sanctuary*, terms he'd picked up from an architectural magazine. Apparently, the thing to strive for was a tension between prospect—meaning the sense of vista, of large open spaces or windows, which intimated that the world was full of possibility that you could aspire toward—and sanctuary, which meant exactly that: small spaces, the safety of beds or bookshelves or chairs, the slope of attics. Too much of one, you lost the feeling of home, of somewhere you, in your limited self, could live day-to-day; too much of the other, you were stifled by your ordinariness. I disliked us both, a little, sitting at my kitchen table with our coffee and sweets, thinking on what we required from our lives, or at least thought we had a right to hope for, though we wouldn't get it, no one did, not even the people in the magazines.

"That one," he said, showing me on his phone. "That's the one."

A brick house, with the sun behind it. Woods. Fields. A creek through the woods. Lustrous empty rooms.

"It's beautiful."

"I grew up on a farm," he said, "but the house was nothing like that."

"Where was the farm?"

"Near Goderich."

"Are your parents still there?"

"I think so. I'm not sure if they're still alive."

He got up before I could speak.

"I should get going," he said, "I'm doing Dorothy's groceries today."

"Does she still cook?"

"She never did. Michael was the one who cooked. Now it's just microwave dinners. Michael was a good cook. I knew him first. Before I knew Dorothy."

I saw his face, and I understood, or rather, I made a leap, guessing, and decided my guess was true, but since I didn't ask, I couldn't be sure.

I had an aunt, or a great aunt, my mother's aunt, who had been the mistress of a man she worked for who was much older. She was from a generation that used words like *mistress* unselfconsciously, as preposterous to me as my having a wife would have been to her.

When he died, she took care of his wife. They'd known each other, of course, in some way, perhaps only in passing, perhaps more frankly. It's so easy to assume simplicity or naïveté in people now dead, because they didn't speak about themselves the way we do, or at least the way we try to, or wish to.

I don't know what the man's wife did or didn't know, but my aunt looked after her when she could no longer look after herself. Visited her in the care home, presumably sat with her listening to the television, training her own eyes toward where the wife looked, though she looked nowhere, staring at a spot on the opposite wall. My mother thought it was horrible, and I didn't think much about it at all; I was a young woman when my aunt died. I'd found straight people boring, even comic, part of a long list of things that didn't interest me. The wife had been dead a long time by then.

I thought of this aunt more often these days, not as someone I now admired, not saintly or self-sacrificing. Just someone who continued doggedly in the circumstances they found themselves in, who saw their lives through as best they could. I think Roger must have imagined he had a duty to see Dorothy through. Until he stopped imagining that, realizing that duty is a thing you can walk away from and not suffer very much, not as much as you thought you would.

Washing the cups, I wondered if I could work up the nerve to ask him about Dorothy's husband. I decided not to risk the humiliation of being wrong. I pictured Roger as a younger man, and the relationship that is so outlandish, so outside the vocabulary of anyone who would have known Dorothy or her husband, that not much effort would be required to conceal it. There are certain advantages to invisibility. None of this was necessarily more than my imagination, but I'd settled it before I'd finished wiping the counter.

The next week Roger texted me a picture of the brick farmhouse with a SOLD sign in front of it. Roger stood beside the sign, smiling, gesturing to the bold black letters.

He came to see me before he moved away. He brought beautiful macaroons from one of the new cafés, most of which weren't actually new. He laughed at himself, browned shavings of coconut crumbling over the kitchen table, saying he was going to love everything, now that he was leaving, even the hipster enclaves that made him feel old.

"Could you check on Dorothy sometimes?"

"She doesn't know who I am."

"Bring Emma. She'll remember Emma. Or she'll like Emma, anyway."

I wanted to say that he didn't know me very well, that he ought to have someone else who he could ask, that it was astonishing that he didn't have anyone else to ask, that if he wanted to check on Dorothy he could make the drive himself, that Dorothy was not my problem, that I had chosen my loyalties (Robin, Emma), I had no room for other ones.

It was late March before I first went to see Dorothy. Emma ran ahead. The earrings in my hand, in a little gold box.

I could smell inside the house from the porch. Mould, wet-cat smell of old body, neglected plumbing, mouse nests.

She opened the door. Her hair was thinner than I remembered. She wore a blue nightgown, a purple bathrobe with a trailing cord. She kept one hand on the handle, prepared to shut us out.

"Dorothy?"

"Yes? What is it?"

"I'm a friend of Roger's. This is my daughter, Emma. We met?"

"Oh Roger," she said. "Yes, come in. Come in. You can leave your shoes on, if you like."

The squalor inside was worse than the smell and seemed sadder because the house otherwise looked like mine. Narrow hall, front room to the right, doorway to a dining room, kitchen at the back, narrow stairs beside the doorway, presumably the same bathroom and three bedrooms upstairs. She fiddled with the cord of her robe without managing to tie it, moved toward the living room, knocking books and magazines from the couch to the floor and gesturing for us to sit. Emma, who had a cold and couldn't smell, prowled: several huge vases of dried grass and peacock feathers, stacks of both clean and dirty plates on a big table against the wall, open cardboard boxes, as though Dorothy was in the middle of packing up, attempting to establish some order or to get rid of things. There was a wet patch on the ceiling, a pot under it that caught the drips. Roger had fled from this.

I wanted to take Emma and leave, but I smiled at Dorothy, sitting at the other end of the couch. She drew her robe around herself.

"Roger asked me to see how you were."

"Oh, I'm fine, I'm fine. A little…you know, a little tired. Not at my peak. But Roger calls. He tells me the news. And he'll be back soon."

She thrust her hand out at the room.

"A bit of a mess. But he'll help when he gets back."

If she believed he would come back, it was not my tragedy. If he had told her he would, it was not my fault.

"I brought you these," I said, drawing out the little box. "You lent them to me."

She politely opened the box.

"Oh, those are very pretty. But it's a mistake. They aren't mine."

"You gave them to me," I said.

"I can't have. They aren't mine."

She handed back the box. I put it in my pocket.

The room was growing dark. Dorothy shuffled to the light switch. There were dead flies in the glass shade of the overhead fixture, but the room was improved. I could feel heat coming from the vent by my feet. Glancing into the kitchen, I saw cans, boxes of instant noodles in the open cupboards. She must be used to the smell, I thought. She had food. She must have money for heating bills and she remembered to pay them. There was a life here, her life. I didn't want to demean her by thinking her entirely wretched. I remembered our real estate agent chirping about the amount of work our house would need to *make it livable*, as though the old woman who had died in the kitchen hadn't lived there for fifty years, had not, in fact, been real. Though we had ripped out the greasy carpets, refinished the floors, replaced the windows, so we must have, in some way, thought that too.

There was a photograph on the wall opposite: a man in a grey sweater, laughing on a deck overlooking a lake, a tall man, maybe fifty, his glass raised to toast whoever was taking the picture. Dorothy. Roger.

I spent the next several weeks feeling I ought to do something, and not knowing what it was. I composed unsent texts to Roger, I ranted to Robin, who told me I was not in a position to take care of an old woman who didn't know me or trust me. I said I should call someone, but Robin reminded me that there was no one to call, and anyway, Dorothy had not asked for help. What forces of the benevolent welfare state could I conjure that were more than a figment of my liberal imagination?

Once I brought Dorothy groceries, but she didn't answer the door, and I left the bags on her porch, with a note. When I passed the house the next day, they'd been taken inside.

In the later spring, when the leaves were fully out, Dorothy died. Roger came back to arrange the funeral and deal with the house, which had been left to her younger sister, who lived in Manitoba and was unable to travel. I helped Roger with the garage sale, going over in the evenings to sort and throw away. After the garage sale I invited Roger home. The sale had gone well, attended mostly by the older Portuguese and Brazilian neighbours who'd been friendly with her, in spite of not really having a language in common. The women stood firmly in their flowered dresses, their flat black shoes, arms and shoulders monumental. Secure in themselves, even as I thought the world they'd known was vanishing, or already vanished. But it's not as simple as that, as one world giving way to another. I needed to stop imagining I knew the truth about strangers.

I watched as they picked over the necklaces and dishes. I wondered about the photograph of the man on the porch, whether Roger had taken it, would hang it in his new house, looking at the face, allowing himself the illusion the photograph offered: the past as a perfect moment of joy, raised glass, laughter, rippled lake. I stood with the metal cash box, Robin beside me, not sure how to be useful, sometimes touching my waist, which, I imagined, was abhorrent to the old women. But they smiled at Emma, stroked her hair with proprietary zeal, smiling on me as a mother. Perhaps they understood everything, and minded nothing, because not many people actually care very much, one way or another, how someone else lives.

Roger told me he'd made a mistake. The farm was isolated, the garden too much to manage on his own. His friends did not visit often; it turned out the farm was still too far from the city. He sometimes drove to a café that had recently opened in the nearest town, run by a couple from Montreal. He read, but there were so many hours in the day. He should never have moved in winter: digging the car out, the cold at night seeping through every fingerling gap in the old walls of the house as he struggled with the covers, imagining the tap of a branch against the window was a knock on the door, remembering his grandmother's belief in the Banshee's knock. He laughed, and then quickly stopped laughing, thinking, I hoped, of Dorothy, lying in her bed, listening, thinking she heard a knock, hearing a knock.

THE FETCH

Everyone believes in ghosts.

Very few people say they do, but hasn't everyone had at least one moment when, standing alone in a room, they have felt eyes looking at them? Even as they insist they are undivided and purposeful, they have felt, close at hand, a shadow-companion, watching.

Everyone believes in ghosts.

I have been, I admit, very nervous lately. I am married to a woman some decades younger than myself and feel the anxiety of gradual inadequacy. My wife is beautiful, accomplished, just hitting her stride. When we met she was a graduate student (not mine—I have standards), a young friend of my then-wife who was a cultivator of ambitious young women. She came to our house for dinner and met our children, and she was unsure and enchantingly self-absorbed and shortly after guilt-ridden and touchingly dependent on me. And I— at the height of my success, and seen by her to be wiser and more vital, more assured and curious than I probably was—I was briefly a remarkable man.

Ten years later I find myself shabby, my lustre temporary, my lust rebuked, my reputation faded, and my academic pursuits pompous and verbose. I am out of date. Nadia has transformed herself into a stylish woman of thirty-four with razor-sharp black hair, a woman unencumbered by children, who wears spike-heeled leather boots to faculty meetings and cultivates a reputation for professorial daring. The whisper of her skirt promises to revitalize the history department, to make it modern and current, and in an epoch of hysterical infatuation with contemporary relevance, no one seems to regard this as a contradiction in terms. She leads me by the arm at her various functions, where no one has heard of me. I suppose in a marriage (this is my experience anyway) one eats the other, but is it fair that she should eat me? I don't have much time left. She does. I spend my last days swallowed up by her marvellous narcissism. She doesn't love me anymore. If she did I could bear everything else.

I am, technically speaking, a senior citizen. Last week a young woman offered me her seat on the subway, and I was so appalled that I sat down. I am no longer interestingly older; I am just old. This sudden realization of sexual irrelevance came winging at me hand in hand with the knowledge that I am so near death he is *looking* at me (through binoculars probably, though our houses are close together). Anyone in my position would be nervous.

Staring in the mirror I find myself grim and dilapidated. The bleached skull begins to show, the skin stretches paper-dry. Women find me distasteful. And I am dying, something I was not prepared for. Said like that, how idiotic! How obvious! What did I think was going to happen?

Foresight has never been my strong suit. I have been married six times. I loved each one of my wives and they loved me. We were happy for a while, all of us. I have children from the first five marriages. Nadia does not want children. I suppose I should be relieved, but I'm not. We are so tenuously linked that nothing holds us. Perhaps children would. Or maybe I just want something else to hold me down. I'm like a balloon with a man's face scribbled on it—I need something to tether me to the world for a little longer.

I am alone, most days, in our empty house. I retired to write, but it seems I have really retired to putter, checking the windows, jumping at sounds that have no source. When I go into my study other people's books frown down at me.

There is a man living next door. He moved in three weeks ago last Tuesday. We have not met, and I must stave off the moment when we do—if we see each other face to face, it's all over. I've seen the side of his head, thinning grey hair, stooped shoulders, the scar on the back of his neck revealed as he bent his head. I ducked behind the curtains, my heart like a hooked fish, because I recognized him. Stationed in my living room, I considered my next move. I must beware this new neighbour. He is not an enemy, not a rival, no, no, no, no: *this man is myself.*

I have not mentioned this to Nadia. She would recommend doctors and pills and be kind, courtesy masking her contempt.

The first time I married, in the early sixties, I married a woman named Elaine Schwartz. When we met, Elaine was studying folklore. Her long hair was curly and oily and dark, and she wore cotton dresses she made herself. She published poetry in small, high-minded periodicals and talked about cultivating a mythological consciousness. She told me about the Fetch. I thought she was only anthropologically interested, but she said her grandmother had seen her own Fetch before she died. She told me the story of Percy Bysshe Shelley walking along the empty Italian beach the week he drowned. He met his double, blue-lipped, seaweed salting through matted hair and torn clothing, and his double fixed him with a glittering eye and asked, "How long do you mean to be content?" And Shelley knew his number was up, because Shelley was the kind of man who had lived his life among ghosts and would know one for what it was and not waste time on explanations. I imagine that when the wind came up and the sky darkened around the small boat that destroyed him, Shelley saw, in the rising water, the face of his double, mouthing words in the green darkness, and felt, underneath his fear, a completion. Poetry right up to the end.

A Fetch is a double that appears as a harbinger of death. The Fetch is a very old superstition, and while the name is Irish in origin, versions are told all over the world. The creature has many names, but Elaine liked the name Fetch best and so do I. This creature comes to fetch you—though the dreadful questions are: Where? And to what?

I have not spoken to Elaine in some time, though we keep in touch. She lives near Kingston and talks to ghosts. She is old now and complains sometimes that there is no one to take care of her, though our three children visit her often, and our eldest, Isabel, lives close by and is devoted to her, whereas she barely speaks to me. But Elaine has other visitors. Banshees, White Hands, Black Dogs, Herne the Hunter, the Erlking. Beloved ghosts as well, like her parents and her sister. They speak to her as she walks the house at night. When she told me this I thought she was crazy. Now I know better.

But I will not wait for my Fetch to come and fetch me. I will seek him out.

His name, I discovered from stealing his mail, is Harold. Not very ghostly, I admit.

On Thursday, after watching his car pull out of the driveway, I broke into his house. Even his driving is familiar—cautious, at odds with the red of the sports car. I would have expected him to drive something worthier, more battered. I shuddered, couldn't help it—the car was in such bad taste. Then I went around through the yard and opened the back door. Unlocked, which in itself argues supernatural origin. Does any human in Toronto leave their door unlocked?

His kitchen is yellow, clean except for a coffee cup set on the counter in the exact position I'd set mine ten minutes earlier. I had no plan. Was there some kind of proper protocol? I should have phoned Elaine; she would have understood. I pictured her on the phone, sighing, at once vague and attentive, her free hand twisting her long grey braid. And thinking of her, I remembered what she said about the significance of objects. To have power over an enemy, you must get hold of something precious to him. Toenail clippings. Hair. Cherished possessions. In the bathroom, taking out my clean handkerchief, I detached three hairs from his comb and wrapped them up. They were white and soft and made me nauseous. Then I went into the bedroom to find his books. The really loved books would be near his bed, like mine were. More personal even than hair or fingernails.

The bedroom was nautically neat, blue and white with an iron-frame single bed, sheets hotel-crisp, a quilt overtop. One plain white bookshelf beside a small desk. The room dismayed me. It was so unlike mine, so much the room of a single man, lonely and fastidious. All my bedrooms have been messy, a battleground between myself and my wives, rife with disorder, the dingy sheets and carelessness of a shared territory, sad accumulations of dust and underclothes marking the slow death of desire, even the desire to please. Standing there, the quietness so restorative, I lay down on the bed, looking at the books, envying my double his restrained life.

His books were disappointing. Nothing theoretical or literary here, nothing published before 1950, nothing containing an index. I was not wrong about the naval feel of the room: there were several books about boats, coffee-table books with the kind of coated paper that blinds you when the light strikes it. And a whole set of Patrick O'Brian, cloth-bound covers with gold lettering. These books were loved. Soft limp spines, stained pages, pressed items falling out when I shook them. Random bookmarks, postcards, scribbled phone numbers on scrap paper. One postcard had a picture of a cathedral and on the other side in thick looping handwriting: *Gothic spires and grotesques! Took a hundred years to build! Think it was worth it? Wish you were here. Really.* No signature. I put that in my pocket.

I wanted one more thing. Something small and light, but memorable, something he would miss at once and be unsettled by. Getting up from his bed, my head ached. There was a pain in my arm, and I steadied myself against the wall. A little figure carved in stained dark wood stood on the bedside table, a man, bent, leaning on a staff, one hand raised. It could have been a saint or *Lord of the Rings* memorabilia, but whatever it was I took it and bolted, nearly falling down his stairs, and left the back door swinging open.

In my study, I arranged the wooden man and the postcard and the hairs on my desk. The three hairs sat at the feet of the little figure like an offering, with the card propped up behind. Then, like a good thief, I rested.

"Harold's house was broken into today."

"Harold?" I said with expert innocence. Nadia paused, forking up her food.

"Harold. The new neighbour. I thought you met him."

"I didn't. I didn't know you had."

We both chewed for a time.

"I don't like the idea of you working here alone all day."

This touched me. Not her concern, but her pretense that I was working.

"Think of you up there, on the top floor. You might not even hear someone come in."

I scraped my fork across the plate to annoy her. "What is Harold like?"

"I don't know. Nice. He speaks very quickly, but he was pretty shaken up. He said the only thing they took was a carved figure from the bedroom. It's small, but very valuable.

Belonged to his great-grandfather. So he thinks they knew what they were doing. Professionals. That made me worried."

I kept eating, stung by my wife's wilful imperceptions. How could she be so blind to the nature of our neighbour? Was she only pretending not to notice? What if they were in league? I excused myself hurriedly. She assumed my stomach was upset and made foul herb tea. Her competence is infuriating.

That night, I left Nadia sleeping and went downstairs to sit at the kitchen table and eat crackers. Light spilled from his kitchen window also. What did he think of, in the middle of the night? If we, he and I, could sit and talk, I would have some serious questions. Atheist, comfortable, arbitrarily left-wing, born too young for any wars, I've had no stand to take, no battle to pitch, or rather, my stands and my battles now strike me as ephemeral—complicated demands made by desire, nothing more. What are my effects, my marks of permanence? A list of scholarly articles, a slim book on the work of Emmanuel Levinas, and another on Maurice Blanchot's view of the work of Levinas, both men bearing such a contingent and diffuse notion of the self that I find myself wishing for the kind of pugnacious assertion of personality I like to think my ancestors had. But my ancestors could not have seen the end result: me—in my renovated Victorian house with my sixth wife asleep upstairs—sitting at a table made of salvaged barn-board eating crackers out of a box and (yes, I held my hand to my face, it came away wet) weeping for the commonplace waste of my life. The sight might have discouraged them. And it was discouraging—the night, the glowing face of the clock above the stove, the overwhelming welter of all my days pressing on me without coherence.

My wives, of course, provide some kind of chronology. I listed them on my damp fingers. Elaine, the folklorist, companion of my youth, who increasingly does not bathe and who could advise me now. Sarah, who wanted to be a more successful actress than her talent and my time allowed and who left me almost immediately, taking with her our young daughter. Maggie, who smoked clove cigarettes and wrote pretty good novels and drank with the low-level persistence of the true alcoholic, Maggie who was as tall as I was and sarcastic and crass and passionate about labour rights but who still insisted on sending our twin sons to private school, Maggie who left me for a woman who taught at the school, with whom she still lives and who my boys call Mama, though they call me by my first name. Then there was Claire, a melancholy poet who died in a whiteout on the highway, her car clipping the side of an eighteen-wheeler that must have risen up out of the snow like an iceberg, who left me with a flourishing career and a two-year-old daughter, for whom I had to hire nannies, but what else could I have done? My daughter says these women were entirely hostile to her, which can't have been true. And Hannah, lovely Hannah, who ended my daughter's unhappiness, who cooked, who collected textiles and was willing to stay at home and read aloud to our children (she bore three and loved

Claire's just the same) and made our house a chaotic hand-printed scratched warren of demonstrative love, and managed to emerge still beautiful and funny until I left her, when I was already old. She stood in the kitchen with a wooden spoon in one hand and shook with anger and said, "You've made a fool of me." She did look foolish just then, like one of those women you see on the street who you can tell at a glance is barely protected from madness by a thin layer of money and successful children and a house with a vegetable and wildflower garden shaded by old trees. Protected, but still unmoored, bulky, useless, not aging well. She thought she was anchored, and I cut her loose like it was easy. It wasn't, but it couldn't be helped.

Now I live in a smaller house with no mess, in which everything is intentional. I eat crackers alone in the middle of the night and look at the surfaces on which dust is not permitted to gather. We do not really live in this house. We rest lightly on it, and a cleaning lady comes once a week and wipes away our traces. I fight this a little. I leave things on the floor and I clog the sink with hair and I bear Nadia's dislike when she says the toilet seat is disgusting, but it's an uphill slog.

Outside, the night settled into deeper darkness as his kitchen light went out.

I broke in again the next morning. I knew he would lock his door now, so I settled on the basement window as my way in. The window is in the walkway between our houses, not visible from the street, easy to force without breaking. Our houses are copies of each other, city twins still identical after years of renovation. I went in feet first, wiggling, and after some anxious moments I was standing in his basement, grey light seeping in through the open window.

I found a light switch but the bulb was burnt out. As my eyes adjusted to the shadows I saw an unfinished concrete bunker full of boxes and filing cabinets and old rugs. A chair here and there. The furnace hulking in one corner, not yet turned on, even though it was growing cold. The boxes overwhelmed me. What had he carried into a new house only to shove summarily into a damp basement? The boxes smelled of mildew. I felt my way up the stairs, meaning to take something from the kitchen and let myself out the back door.

The basement door was locked from the other side. Stumped, I felt my way back down the stairs and sat on one of the broken chairs, which wobbled under me. I looked around. There didn't seem to be much worth taking, certainly not much that he would notice, and anyway, I needed to turn my attention to getting back out, which might prove very difficult. I stood up, striking my head on the low ceiling, and sat back down, sweating like a pig. But the whack to my head gave me clarity, and as I blinked through the pain I decided to empty out the boxes. That would unnerve him.

They were full of paper. Sorted and labelled. As a scholar I paused, struck by the cruelty of what I was about to do. But I turned over the first box, and the bundled sheets fell out with a satisfying anarchic whoosh and settled around my feet. I picked up a few pages and stuffed them between my undershirt and shirt, where they crinkled and poked, then moved on to the next box until I had emptied four, taking a few pieces of paper from each one so that I rustled when I moved. The boxes were surprisingly heavy.

I heard the front door open, heard steps in the hall above me. I edged my way to the open window. Steps passed back and forth overhead, water ran. Then a humming sound, as though he'd turned on the radio or was talking to himself.

I moved slowly, like someone in a nightmare, pulling the chair closer to me. It caught on something, and I watched as a stack of boxes, dislodged by the chair leg, slumped over loudly and lay on top of the snowstorm of released paper.

Silence above me, listening, then steps to the top of the stairs.

"Hello?"

The voice on the other side of the door was a fearful whisper. I grabbed the chair and climbed onto it, my arms reaching through the open window.

"Hello?" The voice was louder now.

He was brave, I had to give him that. I struggled, pulling myself up.

Behind me, the basement door opened. I didn't look back but wheezed my way through, fighting free of the window and up into the walkway as he came down the stairs. I shut the window as he stumbled over the mess I'd left for him and was in my own house peering through my living room curtains by the time he ran out his front door and looked wildly down the street.

And so another night in which I sat awake, this time with his papers spread out in front of me. Some were handwritten, some typed, and the most recent printed. They were all different parts of a breathlessly mediocre seafaring novel.

Shouting against the howling wind, he staggered blindly across the deck and grasped the rigging, clinging like a rat. He could not tell if the terrible pounding in his ears came from the storm or from the thudding of his heart. Dread filled him. He knew suddenly that the storm was not the only horror to be faced that night. Gasping, he implored the heavens, casting his eyes skyward as if for any glimpse of moon or stars, anything to pierce the darkness, the rising wall of black water. His jacket and shirt clung to him like a cold, dead skin. Falling silent, he seemed to hear in the wind a voice, calling over and over a word he knew to be his own name. As a great wave crashed over him, nearly washing him away, he turned and saw a sight that brought home to him all he was most reluctant to know. Hanging on for dear life, he found himself at last face to face with—

I searched, but could not find the rest of the passage, and sat at my desk, shivering. I pictured my double lying awake in the darkness in his narrow bed, wondering who was persecuting him and why, mourning the destruction of his much-drafted, unsuccessful work. I felt such kinship, such compassion, thinking of his folly, his failure, his naked vanity and misplaced need. We were joined—both graspers at straws, and the water closing over our heads. I folded up the pages and put them carefully behind the postcard.

All folktales, all superstitions, Elaine would tell you, rest on the rule of three: three sisters, three brothers, three spells, three chances, three perils, three apparently impossible tasks. I knew I had to go back one more time. Persistent and methodical, I would smash his kitchen window. I knew what I needed: a towel, a hammer, and a container of lard.

This last may seem absurd, but I'd read it in a novel and it was sound advice. The hero, executing a break-in into an archive, packs lard, hammer, and towel. He spreads the window with lard, lays the towel over it, and smashes the window. The lard makes the glass stick to the towel so it comes away easily, and the towel lessens the sound of the breaking glass, which was important since I intended to do this in the middle of the day.

Nadia is the kind of woman interested in slow food and local eating. She buys whole, though small, pigs at farmers' markets and reduces or reconfigures them in some baroque way in our industrial-quality oven. I eat well, though the constant detailing, the relentless authenticity, can be very tiring. Nothing passes the threshold of this house that is not artisanal, and the whole effect is somewhat self-conscious. However, it is useful if you need to find a bucket of high-quality lard on the bottom shelf of your fridge, even if Crisco would have worked just as well.

Fictional description makes everything sound so simple. The lard got all over my hands and my clothes. The towel kept slipping off one corner. The cloth masked the sound only slightly. Shards of glass still clung stubbornly to the sill. I bundled the towel in a bag.

His kitchen was shipshape. I washed my hands at the sink and stood for a moment, admiring a picture on the wall. Not a picture exactly, but a beautiful print of a blue square. Just blue. Not even a variance in shade. Sky, or sea, or what I hoped the end might look like. Blue, forever.

Upstairs, I lay down on the bed and looked at the ceiling. It was one of those wavy plaster ceilings, flecked waves curving into a circle. I shifted, my arm hurting me, and found I was staring into the friendly face of a small black terrier. I hadn't known Harold owned a dog.

"Good boy."

His ears went up. I offered my fingers and he licked them, possibly tasting traces of lard, and I saw a row of little spiked teeth.

I didn't mean to fall asleep. In the late afternoon light I woke to the sound of barking downstairs. I heard Harold exclaim in surprise at the sight of the dog, and as I fell out of bed I knew what the dog was and why it was a black dog and I caught sight of my own face in the oval mirror and saw the wreck of my hair and the pale folds of my skin and I ran down the stairs, grabbing a spoon from the dish rack as I passed, and climbed out the broken window, cutting my leg on a long shard of glass. Harold came after me (out his own back door) yelling, with the dog behind him barking joyously.

I scrambled over the fence into my backyard and saw Nadia's car pulling into our garage from the alley behind our house. I ran to the front, Harold still yelling behind me, behind him the dog, and behind the dog, Nadia, confused and stumbling. I reached the front lawn, trailing blood.

I was almost at my own stairs when I felt a pain in my chest, a pain large enough that I had to stop running, and I toppled down into the warm grass. The pain grew larger, darker, condensing itself in my chest. The black dog was licking one of my ears enthusiastically, and I saw my Fetch bending over me, staring right into my face, exactly me, in his eyes my fear and my regrets, and behind him Nadia, her beautiful face warped with love and grief, and behind her a perfect sweep of blue, just as I had hoped.

ACROBAT

Zoë fell in love with an acrobat because of the dragon tattooed across his shoulders and because of the way his teeth were crooked and because of the wild nest of his hair.

Eleven years old: cynicism, nervous hope in a thicket of expectation. Her flesh unfamiliar almost overnight, her own hair tufted like a squirrel's tail.

Circus Festival
July 20th
Fire breathing! Acrobats! Juggling!
Performance 8:00 p.m
Free workshop for ages 8-12 from 2-4 p.m
Registration not required

In the picture, a dark green dragon, red tendrils of smoke curling from flared nostrils, red block letters. Her mother saw the sign in the library, her mother who was forever trying to get her out of the house.

That was the summer they moved from the blue house in Thunder Bay to the greyish yellow bungalow in Bracebridge with a front yard of concrete and dying grass. Zoë's mother had announced a year earlier, "I deserve a new start," following a period in which she'd barricaded herself in a corner of the kitchen, working her way through a pile of self-help books, pausing to light cigarettes and look around at the linoleum and dirty windows, evidence of the old life she was resolved to cast away. Zoë heard her parents arguing at night, her mother strident, her father ground to silence, and imagined her mother sealing food in freezer bags, her father at the table staring compliantly at his hands—until finally he gave in and looked for another job, and they loaded the car and drove down the highway. The action of moving galvanized her mother, while her father stepped back into the modest space he had always occupied, tired, willing, often gone. He worked the night shift and slept through the days, and Zoë did not miss him, instead watching in wonder as her mother whirled, affecting change in her life with frightening efficiency.

Now Zoë shared a bedroom with her sister. Her mother slept alone in the bigger room. Zoë saw her sprawling across the length of that white bed, luxurious under the duvet. Smoking out the window alone at midnight, watching the stillness of almost-identical lawns. Zoë could smell the smoke as she lay awake in the next room, Linda asleep beside her. They shared a bed; they would get a second bed later when it could be got around to, maybe a bunk bed. There was still painting to do, furniture to assemble, boxes to unpack. Their mother seemed always to be crouched beside a baseboard, her hands spattered with wet paint, her forehead furrowed and beaded with sweat.

"Can I help?"

"Sorry sweetie, not right now. This is something I need to do. Can you do something else?"

Zoë flushed.

"Come on, just for a while, I want to do this alone." She brushed vaguely at the side of Zoë's head with the palm of one hand, turned her back and waited till Zoë left, slamming the door behind her and sitting on the back steps where she could see Linda playing in the yard.

Linda was seven. She still wet the bed sometimes. Zoë would wake up with the sheets damp around her, Linda whimpering. Cleaned up, Linda was pretty in a bug-eyed way and adept at making friends. She could already clamber over the fence in the backyard to where the girl next door waited with a collection of ratty Barbie dolls, their hair fuzzy and their clothes pilled. Zoë watched the two girls, their heads bent over the game in unassailable privacy. She tore up handfuls of dead weeds and gravel and threw them over the fence. They ignored her.

Linda had wet the bed and Zoë hadn't noticed till the morning. She imagined she could still feel something stale and wet clinging to her, and, though she knew she was clean and in fact smelled like soap, it made her ashamed. Her blue shirt was too small, fading to white. Her shorts were yellow and baggy, with grass stains on the seat. Zoë sometimes read her mother's romance novels, which predated the self-help books and had littered the old house. Girls in these books were described as hovering or trembling on the brink of something. Zoë was skeptical. She felt she was slopping over, that an unending humiliation was beginning. Nothing could be more humiliating than a body.

She got to the park early and sat down on a picnic bench. Wasps buzzed around her. She saw him standing by the steps of the bandshell, and she saw the dragon inked blackish green along his shoulders, half-hidden by his dirty under-shirt, which she knew was called a wife-beater, an exciting name, offering a glimpse into an adult world of beer bottles, broken windows, shouting. He was practicing tumbling with another man, younger, slighter. Both of them had pierced ears, were taller and wirier than the men she knew. A third man, with the same whipcord look, his eyes red, stood off to one side, smoking.

The picnic bench was hot beneath her. She dug her fingers into the carved letters scored deep in the green paint. *Ashlie + Jon 4ever, Melissa + Shauna rule.* And in marker, *Ben Scott sucks cock.* "It will be easier when school starts," her mother had promised, giving Zoë a fraught smile. "You'll get to know people if you just make an effort." Zoë watched the men, and they did not watch her.

Slowly more people arrived. A small boy, his mother holding his hand. One of the men told her the boy was too young, the mother frowned and protested, and the boy remained. Two girls Zoë's age, in tank tops and flip-flops, rhinestones on their jeans, one of them showing the beginning of breasts. She held her shoulders back to show them off, whereas Zoë would have slouched to hide them. The other girl's arms were decorated with temporary tattoos, sparkly butterflies that matched the butterfly clips in her hair. Zoë hoped neither of them would look at her. An older boy, alone, bristling and tough, eyed the men and their muscles and their cigarettes with hangdog admiration. Nobody else. Failure hung in the air. Zoë stood up and walked toward the little group, tucking in her chin. She stood beside the small boy. Everyone waited in expectant silence.

"All right, we begin," the dragon man said. The younger man stepped forward, the third man threw his cigarette grandly into some bushes.

The dragon man was barefoot. The light shone through his hair, which made him look like the picture of Jesus in her grandmother's house. Ringed by brightness. He forced a smile. His teeth were yellow, a front one chipped, the incisors prominent as fangs. Smiling, his face creased into tired lines. He was from Montreal, he said, his troupe travelled around to different towns, performing and teaching. He was going to teach them to balance, to tumble, to walk on stilts, and afterwards they could go home and bring their parents to the show, in front of the bandshell. The other two men stepped back deferentially as he talked, keeping their eyes forward, holding still as he bounced on the balls of his feet. He did not ask for any names, or say his own name.

Balance. Without warning, the dragon man squared himself, and the younger man leapt onto his back. He must have climbed but to Zoë he flew, and then the younger man was standing on the dragon man's shoulders like it was nothing. The third man flopped down on the grass, legs held up, and the dragon man made a quick movement that vaulted the younger man through the air and onto the splayed feet of the third. The younger man stood on the tensed feet, swaying. He gripped the wrists of the dragon man and (Zoë couldn't fathom how) was lifted, or flipped himself over, so that he was held straight above the other man's head, hands clasping wrists, the younger man's feet pointed toward the sky. The two men looked into each other's contorted faces, teeth bared, laughing. Then all three unfolded and jumped into a row, nimbly perfect.

Zoë clapped loudly, startling everyone else into clapping too.

The dragon man pointed to Zoë.

"Look, you come with me, and two others with them."

She stepped forward. She could feel a blush across her neck. Her blushes were dark, mottling her skin, her nose reddening more than her cheeks, and the more she fought with her blushes the more they spread.

The dragon man lay down on the grass. He motioned for her to stand beside him. He took her hands by the wrists. She looked away, redder and redder.

"This way you are secure. You can't slip."

She braced herself, as if she might be sprung into the air, able to hold her body straight toward the sky. She waited, wanting to close her eyes. The man manoeuvred her around and placed his spread feet against her stomach, just above the waist.

"Ready?"

She nodded vigorously to show she was not afraid. Without looking at her, he lifted her up, balanced on his feet, holding her wrists. She struggled, her body folding clumsily over his legs.

"Stretch out. Stretch your legs out."

Puffing, she straightened her legs, fighting with what she'd expected, a captivating image of herself lithe and flying. But then she felt it. Her weight shifted, lightened, she lifted across his feet. She'd never been in an airplane, but she thought this must be the moment of leaving the runway—a dizzying liberation in which everything you were fell away from you. But even better, because she wasn't a speck in the innards of a metal bird, this was just herself, changed. She kept very still, wondering, her body now like a flag in the wind.

"See? I told you."

He put her down abruptly. She pulled at the front of her shirt, her heart beating fast. The butterfly girl was still up, thrashing and squealing, and the older boy, pointing his toes.

The dragon man faced her, on his feet again.

"Thanks." She stuck out her hand (wasn't that right?) and flinched as he laughed, her hand wavering in the space between them, and he took it and held it, his own hand warm and dry.

"Come tonight. Come and see the show."

He had his back to her before she could answer, and the girl with the breasts stepped up.

Zoë sat on the grass and watched him. When he moved, the cloth of the wife-beater wrinkled against him. When he lifted his arms, the dragon stretched. The dragon's tail moved up the back of his neck and disappeared into his hair. She looked down.

It was all over very soon. The older boy emerged as the star, able to stand on his hands. Zoë could not even turn a cartwheel. She had tried, over and over in the backyard of their old house, too scared at the last moment to abandon her body to the air. When the men brought out three pairs of small, battered stilts she did not get up but watched as others were strapped in and helped to march across a few feet of grass. When she was asked, she shook her head. The dragon man frowned at her, and she was stricken at disappointing him. But she didn't want the afternoon to end with her lumbering, earthbound, tied into the stilts. She had flown. She didn't want to spoil it. She sat, hugging her knees to her chest, thinking of that flight, the moment already something to be hoarded and revisited and kept secret, a standard against which other things would seem faded.

"All right, we're finished. Come back tonight! Remember. Come back tonight!"

They stood in their line, smiling dismissive smiles as everyone turned and walked away. But across the park she looked back. They were in a circle, talking earnestly, dishevelled with heat and dust. She stood at the park gate, leaning against the black iron railings, willing him to look up, see her, nod. Remember. Come tonight. When they walked out the opposite gate without looking back at her, she went home.

She wanted to change her clothes. It was a show, wasn't it? A show meant a dress. She found her yellow and blue striped dress and tugged it over her head. She found the white sandals that pinched her feet. She looked at herself in the bathroom mirror, trying to widen her eyes and fill out her mouth. The mirror was streaked with soap stains and toothpaste, and her mother had stuck Post-its around the frame, curled and spattered but legible:

Take Control of Your Destiny
I Refuse to Be a Victim
Believe

Have Faith
Learn from Your Mistakes
You Can Do It

Zoë thought maybe she could get herself to look older, less solid. She patted water into her hair, trying to make it lie flat. The water left damp patches among the tufts. She found red barrettes on the bathroom shelf and twisted them in.

Her hair remained bushy, and the cotton dress already hung damp in the heat, bunching around the waist. Her legs were bitten and scratched. She stared at her face, fighting something close to panic. It was too hard to be stuck with the same face, the same badly fitting expression. Maybe if she had a necklace. Maybe if her ears were pierced. No, it wouldn't work, it wouldn't work out, of course not. She pulled out the barrettes and dropped them in the sink. Before she could take the dress off, her mother knocked on the door.

"Baby? Time to go."

Her mother and Linda stood on the porch, both in shorts and T-shirts. Her mother patted Zoë's shoulders.

"Sweetie, you'll boil in that dress."

"It's okay."

Linda ran ahead, Zoë following carefully in her tight shoes, her mother beside her, mouth twitching in what Zoë felt was mockery. It made her walk more slowly, conscious of her own sweaty smell staining under her arms. For her mother it may have been something else. Cautionary fear, the wish to give a warning. Whatever it was, her mouth twitched.

Past lines of identical bungalows and down the slope, past the grocery store, past the tennis court, past the big brick houses with vines girding the windows, past the Salvation Army store that smelled like shoes and stale baby powder. Past the former hotel where, according to a sign put up by the Heritage Committee, American visitors once came every summer and danced in the ballroom. There was a photograph on the sign, black and grey shading into white, showing unsmiling couples, the men in limp suits, the women demure under enormous feathered hats. The front of the building was now a Polish restaurant, the rest a rooming house, and flies buzzed against the shut windows. On they walked, down into the park.

She wanted the park to look different. There should be a tent billowing, noise, crowds, something like her idea of the dancing Americans—lanterns hanging in dark trees with moths battering at their bright glow, popcorn sold from a red and white cart, and music. But the park looked the same. There was the bandshell, the pruned bushes and neat grass, the beds of flowers laid out in listless geometric shapes, white, yellow and pink, petals shrivelling in the sun, which was now low in the sky.

"They keep this park nice," said Zoë's mother, lighting a cigarette. She sucked deeply and waved the smoke away apologetically. "They need to keep it nice, with all the people here in the summer."

A few rows of lawn chairs were set in a half-circle, where a town councillor walked between little knots of families and older couples standing on the outer edges of the makeshift seating. Zoë was already learning to tell who the cottagers were by their canvas shoes, cloth hats, deceptively plain clothes. She caught sight of the two rhinestone girls and looked away.

Two speakers were set on either side of the bandshell, and a man sorted through a pile of electrical cords. The dragon man was nowhere that Zoë could see.

"Is this thing going to start?" asked her mother, as if Zoë would know. "God, the bugs will be out soon, we'll get eaten alive. I don't want to be out late." She led the girls to the back row and flopped down, her hair the same yellowish white as the chair.

Zoë sat reluctantly, perching herself on the edge of her seat where the metal cut into her legs. When she saw him, she would be ready. She watched a woman fighting with her child, a little boy, who grabbed at her, howling, kicking at her legs, his face contorted with fury, snot crusted over his mouth and cheeks. The mother, her face flushed, yelled at him to stop. A group of old people stared frankly, friendly and meddling, their own children grown.

"My goodness," said Zoë's mother, jutting her cigarette in the woman's direction, pursing her mouth. "Some people can't control their kids, just can't do it." She batted at the smoke. "Of course, boys are more work."

The woman slapped her son hard.

The old people murmured, and the boy sat down on the grass, one cheek bright red.

"See!" said the woman, her voice high and nasal. "That's what happens, Ashton. That's what happens."

She walked away from him, one hand rubbing a patch of sunburnt skin on the back of her neck. The boy was quiet, wiping his nose with his dirty hand.

"Poor thing. What a shame." Zoë's mother turned Linda's head away.

Zoë looked at the ground and then, covertly, at the boy. She was disgusted suddenly by her mother's pity, and her disgust made her stomach hurt, an ache she tried to ignore. Later she would remember her mother's pity as contempt and, more than that, relief at having someone to pity. Pity also meant self-satisfaction, a quiver of reassurance: *what a shame.*

The boy got up and trotted to his mother, butting against her legs. She dropped to her knees and put her arms around him, murmuring in his ear.

"That is not good parenting," said her mother. "That is mixed messages." She ground out the cigarette under her heel. Behind her, an old woman glanced at the butt, at her mother's bleached hair and long pale legs, flip-flops dangling off her pink-nailed toes. The woman's wrists were slung with thick silver bangles, her face conveying the same dismissal Zoë's mother had for the mixed-message slap. Her mother was wrong about the new start. There was a hierarchy of good fortune that her mother could not subvert. Her mother would manage, she would get through, but Zoë knew, right then, that what she wished for would not happen. She would always be in the same place. Not on the lowest rung, but fairly far down looking peevishly up.

Then Zoë saw him, standing to one side of the bandshell. He was talking to the man setting up the speakers. He now wore a green leotard and a green pointed cap with ear-like flaps sewn onto the sides. A ridged tail wound down from his back, brushing the grass. He and the technician were arguing. Gesturing, the dragon man turned and walked over to where the other two men were standing behind the bushes, out of sight of the audience.

She made herself move, walking toward him faster than she could think and with no idea what she wanted to say. Some words that would let him know that this was something she would remember and be grateful for, that would make him glad she was there. He would see that to her this was more than the disappointing trickle of people, the parched parkland and open sky, and that she, too, was more than those things. She would make him happy.

When she reached him, he shook his head.

"We begin in a minute, you should sit down."

He didn't recognize her. She waited, not able to believe it, but when he waved her away with less patience, she walked off, crouching down on the other side of the bushes, watching the men through the branches.

His tattoo was just visible under the cap. The older man turned away, stood on his hands, his feet pointed into the air. As the speakers grumbled and then roared into life, as music began, as the people moved into their seats, Zoë watched the dragon man.

Her head filled with the sound of the music, distorted by the old speakers. The dragon man shrugged. It was partly an easing of his shoulders, but also a willed disdain setting him apart from his surroundings, as if anything disheartening had nothing to do with him. He remained superior and extraordinary. He grinned at the younger man, whose smile widened, he touched the younger man's wrist, just brushing the skin with his fingers, and then he kissed him, gently and briefly, his fingers still running in a line up and down the inside of the other man's wrist. They both laughed, a breath of a laugh that was more private than anything she'd ever seen or been able to imagine. Surprise jolted her, that unplanned weightlessness overtaking her and making her own body and the air around her strange. A depth and a lightness. Flying.

LONG TERM CARE

Everyone agreed that there was nothing else to be done. He was ninety, and it should have been done a decade ago. He would have his own room. He would eat dinner in the dining room, hunched over his plate, scattering food on the synthetic aquamarine tablecloth, disturbing the plastic carnations in the white vase. He could go for walks around the parking lot on warm days. They would visit.

The final straw had been that day in the bathroom. Elisabeth had let herself in with her own key, because it was Wednesday, and she came on Wednesdays and Fridays and Sundays, with Max and Britta alternating throughout the rest of the week. She came more frequently, it was understood, because Max and Britta each had their own families, children, a web of irrefutable obligations that she did not have. This was a shame, people said, because she was a nice woman. A little heavy, a little earnest, and often flushed in the face, but very kind. Look how good she was to her father.

The house seemed darker than usual, because of the overcast sky, the rain. She stood on the dirty hall mat and took off her glasses, wiping them with the damp cuff of her shirt. Her eyes blurry, her glasses in her hand, going further in, she heard a tap running and saw water flowing out from under the bathroom door (she had moved him entirely downstairs the month before, the bathroom installed, the upper floors given over to storage).

"Papa?"

She had come ready to help him with his bath. She had new soap in her bag, wrapped in purple plastic, soap the doctor said would not irritate her father's skin. Clutching the bag, her raincoat still hanging wet around her, she pushed open the bathroom door.

He was on the floor, naked, water running in streams around his body, streaked pink in the heat, his chin resting on the side of the tub.

"I thought I should get in the bath. I thought—"

She stepped over him and turned off the tap. Then she draped him in a towel, keeping her eyes away from the numbers along his arm and from his penis, vulnerable and comic.

"Couldn't you have waited?"

She heaved him to a sitting position against the tub. He straightened his back and frowned.

"I got sick of waiting."

Elisabeth wasn't late, but she didn't protest the imperious growl, the feeble stab at authority from a man who'd outlived his own importance.

"You kept me *waiting*."

She sat down beside him on the floor, her raincoat falling open, the puddle of warm water soaking her clothes. Both of them looked up absently like strangers sitting on the subway, careful, not touching.

"What are we going to do with you?"

Max and Britta took over. Both knew whom to ask, knew how to organize and take charge, how to devise a plan of action and follow it through. "The important thing," Britta said, "is to make decisions. It only makes it more difficult for him if we leave too much to the last minute or can't make up our minds." Elisabeth was prone to wavering, they all knew this, so she stood aside and let them swap lists and make phone calls. The Home was nearby, suitably expensive, in fact exorbitant, but Max would pay most of it. A well-known colleague of their father's had lived out his last years there, and his children spoke highly of the staff. There was a resident doctor on call in the long term care section, and the doctor spoke excellent German, as did one of the nurses. They felt this might please their father, who in the last decade had often slipped back into his original language, grunting irritably when they reminded him that they only spoke English. "Hearing German might be comforting for him," Max said.

The Home presented a fussy, determined cheerfulness, a tendency toward wooden ornaments and mottos scrolled on the wall. "I think this is really the best we can expect," Britta said. Elisabeth looked back over her shoulder at the lobby, decorated for Christmas, and thought this might be true, but wasn't sure.

A spot came up within a few months. Max phoned to tell her. They had agreed they would not sell the house yet. It would be too hard for their father, Max said, and he was so confused now. Slipping, Britta added, as if he stood on a steep slope, just barely keeping his footing, watching as others gave up and fell away into the dark. Which was true.

Elisabeth went alone to a meeting aimed at children (euphemistically called caregivers) whose parents had recently been resettled into these supervised apartments. There were cookies, sandwiches, coffee so weak the light shone through it. A woman accidentally knocked Elisabeth's arm and her coffee sloshed onto the carpet, and while she helped Elisabeth clean up the woman told her in a tone of conspiratorial complaint that she found it hard to think of her parents as old. Elisabeth didn't know how to answer, since she'd always thought of her father, forty-five when she was born, as old, and she was bewildered by the clarity of the woman's self-pity.

The apartment was carpeted in pale blue (Elisabeth was dismayed on his behalf, thinking of the bare wood floors and worn valuable rugs of the house she'd grown up in), with a picture of two swans clamped to the wall, a cubby with a sink and fridge though no stove, a small bathroom with a metal bar so he could lower himself down onto the padded toilet seat. She chose from among his things a single bed, his armchair, a television, a small bookcase, and what she hoped were favourite books, books she remembered him reading, Hegel, Kant, Schiller, Rilke, Schlegel, Heidegger, Thomas Mann. She could not read German and had not read these books even in English. She had tried but most of them bored her, and he had made fun of her instead of being flattered.

When she showed him the bookcase, he ran his hand along its top, then looked down at his fingers, frowning.

"What's wrong?"

"No dust."

"The building is kept very clean," she said, hoping to sound encouraging.

He steadied himself against the wall.

"I don't read now."

He sat down in the armchair and looked at her, as if expecting an answer to what he had said.

"Don't worry if he seems unsettled at first," the staff supervisor, Joan, told Elisabeth when she left him and went downstairs. "It's normal. He'll be right at home soon." Pantsuited and professionally sympathetic, she smiled warmly.

"Let me know if there's anything else we can do."

Elisabeth saw that this was a way of saying goodbye, and left.

She visited as often as before, but now there was very little for her to do. "A whole package," Britta said approvingly. The track lights, the subdued yellow walls, the well-trained attendants who asked him how he was and did not see, as Elisabeth did, that his answering shout of hoarse laughter was not friendliness or senility, but contempt. She brought in a chair for visitors and sat in it. She brought in green plants and set them along the windowsill, and the cups and plates that had been her mother's. She watered the plants. She brought him the food he loved: sausage, ham, heavy rolls, and blocks of Swiss cheese. She brought coffee in an urn, strong and black, and hid the sugar packets in the pocket of a shirt he never wore. He should drink tea, Max and Britta said, echoing the doctor, it would be better for his heart. Seeing him sitting in his chair, Elisabeth didn't see the point of words like better or worse. She knew there was some idea of saving him, saving his energy, saving his strength, but she couldn't understand what he was being saved for. He loved outwitting other people's officious good intentions, smacking his lips over the coffee with more attention than he gave to anything else.

He was no trouble to the staff, besides his insistence on being addressed as Dr. Bendler, which they assumed meant a medical doctor, rather than a professor of philosophy. It was wonderful, Joan said, to see a resident surrounded by so much family. He did not make new friends in the Home, and his old friends were dead in other countries. He was used to being alone. For as long as Elisabeth could remember, he had been a man of colleagues rather than friends. When her mother died, the list of people to invite to the funeral was very long. This made sense, since she'd been born in Toronto and had never left. Elisabeth wondered who would come to her father's funeral, other than his children. She watched him staring out the window at the winter sky and the row of townhouses, and imagined that he inhabited another place, another city, one she had never seen and which he would not describe to her.

On the days she did not visit, she would go to his closed house after work—she taught kindergarten, the children's shrieks and bouts of calculated submission making it both easier and harder that she hadn't had children—and put objects into boxes, incredulous at how much useless junk even an exact and spartan life will accumulate. Max and Britta offered to help, or hire someone, but she said quickly that she was the eldest, it was her job, surprising herself. I sound like him, she thought, seeing the look on their faces.

She sorted through haphazard files and notebooks, she folded up sheets and blankets and clothes. She supposed these would go to Goodwill after the house was sold. She had no idea what to do with his papers, or his books. Who would want them, who would even look at them?

One night a photograph slid from the pages of a book and fell to the floor. Her father as a young man—a young professor in Freiburg when Jews were still allowed to teach—standing in his garden. His first wife was beside him, and their three daughters, ranged in order of size in front of their parents, their dresses rendered light grey. Elisabeth wondered what colour the dresses had been, thinking of pastels, pinks and yellows, matching the ribbons that were tied in the girls' parted hair. Turning the photograph over, she read the names of the wife and daughters written in modern ballpoint blue on the stained back. His handwriting was shaky, as if he had written the names very recently.

The photograph was disappointing. She wanted figures weighed down by foreknowledge, or ignorantly happy. But it was just a photograph. The eldest girl wore glasses, the wife's smile was strained, the middle and youngest daughters had moved so that their faces were blurred. Her father scowled in his customary way, a familiar expression even on the unfamiliar young face. He would always rather have been working. She was confused, then gratified, to see that his scowl preceded the disaster itself. She imagined the scene as a Sunday afternoon—the family arriving home from church. His wife had thought of herself as a Catholic, right through to the very end. This fact had come to Elisabeth from her own mother, who had pieced out parts of the story over years, sharing them secretly with her children. Looking closely, Elisabeth thought she could see a cross on a chain around the wife's rigid neck, though perhaps it was a pendant. She put the photograph in a cardboard box, a box of things she would not show to anyone.

"He was the saddest man I ever met," her mother said. This was after she was sick, her hair coming away in clumps from her mottled skull. They watched the night skyline through the window of the oncology ward. She laughed, her laugh a barking echo of his. "I thought he was romantic."

Their own family photographs were displayed on the wall of her mother's study, not hidden in the pages of books. The recently married couple at a University of Toronto dinner, Elisabeth's mother surprisingly beautiful even in her heavy glasses, her smile showing white strong teeth, her body rigged up in the boxy neatness of the 1950s. Even with the smile, she is serious, relentless in her love: she will demand everything. He is prematurely grey, slovenly, brilliant, ferocious, marrying his best student. Later, she will excuse him, and even later, she will watch him leave the table early to go upstairs and shut the door while she talks to her children and makes them help with the dishes. Her body will sag, her face will soften, she will become sarcastic and funny. She'll think that young woman at the university dinner is a fool. When she grows sick, thinner even than in the photograph except for a distended belly, he will emerge from upstairs and look after her, tender as he had never before been, an astonishment to her, and perhaps to him. A marriage.

Elisabeth took the box home and put it on a shelf beside her bed. When this seemed melodramatic she moved it to another shelf and put books around it. When this also seemed possessive in a way Britta would have called unhealthy (Britta was a therapist, she knew these things) she stuffed it on a high shelf in the closet beside a bag of old hats. That was better.

Sitting with him the next Sunday afternoon, she found herself uneasily silent. He dozed over his coffee, his eyelids puffed and red.

"Are you still here?"

"Should I go?"

"No, no, not if you don't want to."

He smiled as his eyes shut again. A flash of charm immediately receded. She dumped the coffee into the sink, washed out his cup, listened to his breath shuddering through his slack mouth. She put on her coat. He woke up, shaking his head.

"Are you going?"

She kissed his cheek. He put his hand to her face, but let it drop before he touched her. She turned with her hand on the door handle.

"Let me know if you need anything else."

He stared at her wildly, wide awake.

"Don't let them see you go. They are watching for when you go. I know."

"Papa?"

He looked away.

"Papa?"

She came back into the room, waiting for him to look up.

"What do you mean?"

He did not look up.

She didn't know how to speak to him, she never had. When she was much younger, she had stammered sometimes when she talked, and he had had no pity.

"What is it, Papa?"

She shook his shoulder gently.

He looked up, the panic gone.

"Are you still here? You should go. You'll be late."

She left. There was nothing else to do.

Joan waylaid her at reception.

"I wanted to speak to you. I'm a little concerned that your father may be depressed."

Joan's teeth were crooked, her lipstick an unfortunate deep purple that bled into the lines around her mouth. The ineptitude made Elisabeth unexpectedly confident.

"I wouldn't say he's depressed," she said crisply. "I'd say he's old."

Joan paused just long enough to make Elisabeth feel she'd been rude.

"We understand that it's difficult for residents to make this kind of adjustment. And sometimes it's as difficult for the people who've been the primary caregivers. Or even more difficult."

She touched Elisabeth's sleeve.

"We don't have to do anything yet. We just need to watch him. And it's best for everyone if you are aware. That way we're all working together."

"He's—"

"He's also physically very weak. More so than when he first arrived. It's possible he can't continue to live independently."

"Independently?"

"He may need a higher level of supervision. We just need to be responsive to his needs. So that's why it's good for us to have this conversation now."

She paused again.

"Thank you," Elisabeth said finally, feeling she'd missed a cue, contrite. "I can speak to my family."

Elisabeth knew Joan was right. It was pointless, egotistical even, to enter the game and then wish for different rules. Dying must be managed, like everything else.

The only thing her father had ever told her about his time in the camp was that when the Americans came in their tanks, a soldier gave him a cigarette. For years he had longed for a cigarette. Huddled in the barracks beside other men, smelling the vomit and shit of these men (dysentery was rampant), he dreamed of smoking. Because (Elisabeth thought later, poeticizing as he would not have wished her to do) it was a small thing, a small pleasure, something small enough to seem real, something he could bear to think about. Don't think of the wife, the daughters, the work, the former life, think instead of the smallest thing.

But by then he was so sick, he no longer wanted it. Still, he accepted the cigarette, standing dumbly beside the soldier. The soldier wanted them to stand together, two men smoking, and he had felt obliged. He'd smiled at the soldier and inhaled, though the taste in his mouth was awful, and he almost passed out. The soldier was young, he said, younger than he, wanting to feel generous, to put at ease these people who would never be at ease again.

In Elisabeth's mind the two men appear as if in different photographs. The soldier is brightly coloured, his hair is blond, his eyes blue, he is shiny all over, from cap to boots, a recruitment poster, just what Uncle Sam needs—a terrible innocence. The other man, her father, is black and white, a stick figure, a news report, a picture in a book. Thin as wire, with an emptied face.

On Saturday Elisabeth and Max went to Britta's for lunch. Spouses and children were not present. Britta lived in a house in Parkdale, with crown mouldings and strategically exposed brick walls, original plaster skilfully restored. She fed them homemade pasta and offered to open a bottle of wine. It was painful to contemplate selling the house and they deserved a drink. Max was late, running from the car laughing apologies and shouting that his son had the flu. His long coat flapped out behind him and Elisabeth was reminded briefly of a pinched, difficult boy, who had somehow become this ascetically handsome man, so sure of himself that even his apologies were arrogant, with a charm reminiscent of their father's, but less effortless, more instrumental.

Max and Britta praised the work Elisabeth had done, and the praise was sincere. She accepted a second glass of wine, and they were temporarily happy, united. They sat at Britta's big round kitchen table and pushed away their empty plates, and Britta did not get up to clear right away but sat and smiled. Britta was beautiful, dressed in jeans and a red shirt that clung around her, her hair tangling down her back. Elisabeth still marvelled at her sister's beauty, though Britta herself was beginning to struggle with its slow loss, as what had been a birthright became something carefully preserved, in the face of children and time. Max, the youngest, talked about the value of the house and its contents, the process of appraisal, what he would arrange. Everyone was handling everything so well.

Elisabeth ruined it without meaning to. She described the conversation with Joan and, unsurprisingly, Max and Britta agreed that Joan was probably right, maybe they should rethink, should meet with staff. Max wondered if they should move their father to the ground floor, into the long term care section, where the doctor made regular rounds, after all, remember the bath, there was no reason it couldn't happen again, perhaps they were being unrealistic. Then Elisabeth said the thing she had been thinking, walking away down the hall, talking to Joan.

"I think he thinks he's back there. I think he thinks we put him back there."

They looked at her, waiting, not knowing what she meant. She made a loose defeated gesture, pushing something invisible across the table.

"I think he thinks he's in Buchenwald again."

In the silence that followed she saw her mistake. Britta blushed and dropped her eyes. Max stared.

"I don't think that can be true," Max said, his voice reasonable and cautious, a man dealing with women. "You've taken on a lot here, you feel a lot of stress, but I think that's… I think that can't be true."

Britta stood up and cleared away the plates abruptly, slamming them down beside the sink.

"What a horrible thing to say."

She spoke to the wall, her back to Elisabeth, her shoulders lifting as she shook her head.

"What a horrible, horrible thing."

Elisabeth recanted—she didn't think, she didn't want—and they joined in eagerly, not wanting to risk the fight, all agreeing, tearfully, that the situation had put Elisabeth under so much pressure, which could do things to one's thoughts. "It's not your fault, no one thinks it's your fault," Britta said, wiping her eyes. "It must be very hard on you." She squeezed Elisabeth's hand.

Getting up from his chair alone two weeks later, he fell, bruising the side of his face against the bookshelf, one long defined purple line rising as if someone had drawn a marker down his cheek. He was found on the floor, unable to pull himself up. That settled the question for everyone. Elisabeth imagined his fall like a grainy video loop from the home movies of her childhood—silent, saturated, his arms stretched out, grasping air, nothing to stave off the full drop of his own weight against the hostile edges of the world.

He was moved downstairs. Elisabeth did not argue. As she gathered his clothes into a black garbage bag, she remembered Britta, years ago, saying to her, "You have to take control of your life." She had wanted to reply (perhaps self-righteously) that life was to be lived, not controlled, but the evidence for this was scant. When she set Max and Britta, their families, their houses and securities, against the smaller sphere she occupied in undemanding quiet, she didn't have much to show for herself. This gave her pause; she went on packing.

The long term care section was in a separate wing. The doors into it locked from the outside. She had to punch a code into a keypad to make the doors swing ponderously open and then close behind her with a soft click. In the lounge old people sat, most of them in wheelchairs. Some smiled when she came, automatic smiles that took a long time to fade, and some stared at her with stupid cunning, or slumped forward as if searching for something they had dropped. Elisabeth hurried through and along the corridor to her father's room.

The downstairs corridor was lined with linoleum rather than carpet. "For spills," Joan explained. Lights glared. Elisabeth's footfalls echoed as she walked. A strong smell pervaded the corridor and the lounge, the smell of bleach and air freshener, and underneath, the smells that bleach could only mask.

His room had no pictures. Venetian blinds on the windows, a dresser, and a bedside table for his watch, his teeth, and the things she had kept for him though he would not need them anymore. Keys. A wallet. A green ceramic dish holding stray coins. A comb. A tray for mail, his ornate brass letter opener with a handle shaped like a snake's head. The room was too small for all the plants she'd brought. She put

African violets on the dresser, in a bright red porcelain pot, but in spite of her efforts, the room remained blank.

Coming in the late afternoons, she would find him sitting in his one chair or lying in bed. He would raise his head and look at her, drawing his chin down in a slow nod of recognition before looking away.

One night he had a stroke, and in his confusion threw the pot of violets off the dresser. By the time Elisabeth arrived it had been swept up and thrown away, and the garbage bag changed to a new one, shining white. The young doctor described her father's stroke to her. A small stroke, he said. It might even be part of a series so gradual it would be difficult to tell when they had occurred. A patient like this would slowly lose function over time.

That evening he had come to check on her father, addressing him in German. This was usual, and usually her father answered in kind, eventually reminiscing about places they both had visited, generations apart. Her father had shrunk down in the bed and tried to pull away when approached. He made noises, small noises that had no sense. The doctor had pressed the alarm bell just as her father flung the pot at him. The doctor did not take this personally. Her father had not meant anything by it. It was only the sudden impulse of undirected fear, normal under the circumstances.

Her father stayed in bed after that and more or less stopped talking. This was not medical, the doctor explained. Her father probably could still speak but had decided not to. This was not uncommon. Working with the elderly, he had come to believe that going on living, going on making the effort, was largely a matter of will. He knew this was not a popular opinion, but he hoped Elisabeth would value his experience. Elisabeth heard a hint of accusation in his voice, as if even he could not escape moments of annoyance at such irascible frailty, such helplessness. Weakness is irritating, and the dying can't help but be sometimes irritating to the living. Her father slept on and on, a lump in the bed. She sat beside him with nothing to do. What would she do when he was gone? There would be so much time. She had sometimes, privately and in passing, looked forward to his death as the end of a chapter, or at least the end of her exhaustion. He was an exhausting man; it had taken so much of her energy to be his daughter. She had chosen it, she knew—to excuse him, to care for him, to care so much for what he thought. Now that the end was so near, the open door of the event felt diminished—her life afterward going on as before, only lessened.

When he did speak, he spoke German, words she did not understand, often repeated, not meant for her. At first she tried to get him to explain, but he only gripped the sides of his bed, the kind of hospital bed that could be raised and lowered, and looked away, furiously mute, his strings of grey hair hanging limp around his shining head.

One day she heard a scuffle in the corridor and smelled a sweet, bad smell. A nurse was bending over a woman in a wheel-chair, who was struggling with something in her hand.

"Did you have an accident, Mabel?" said the nurse.

The old woman opened her hand, which was covered in shit.

"An accident," said the nurse, her sympathy stern. "Now we need to clean you again. Mabel," she said, loudly, "we're going to clean you."

Mabel began to moan, and the moan grew, becoming the abject howl of a shamed baby.

"Stop it," the nurse said. "Stop it."

It grew dark early. By the time Elisabeth arrived the next day, the light was already fading. One of the nurses was changing the top sheet, expertly working around her father's unresisting body.

"Oh, I'm sorry."

"I won't be long. Sit down."

Elisabeth edged her way past the nurse and sank into the chair. The setting sun lit the room.

"Your father's asleep."

"I can see that."

"He's asleep most days now. I tried speaking German to him yesterday. He used to like that. My mother's from

Munich, I know a little. But this time I think I scared him. Not on purpose."

"No, of course."

"But English doesn't seem to work either, does it?"

"You should speak English to him. His English is very good, he's lived here most of his life."

"You'd be surprised," the nurse said, smiling to soften the correction.

"Surprised?"

"When they get as old as he is. Most of it goes. They can't help it."

The nurse was a pretty woman, almost young. She wore a pink shirt under her uniform. Her blue eyes were kindly, attentive, certain. She reminded Elisabeth of the soldier in the photograph.

She touched the shoulder of Elisabeth's coat as she left.

"He'll be just fine."

"Yes. Thanks."

Elisabeth sat beside her father in the dark. I'm a silly woman, she thought. She should go home soon. It was getting late and she was hungry. Of course he knew he was safe. It was so obviously true. I'm being neurotic, she thought. This seemed more official, more persuasive, than simply silly. These sealed windows and lights and clean beds and the pleasant doctor, the nurse—what could he be afraid of? Her stupid delusions, her grandiose sense of significance. Horrible to think, as Britta had said. She should stop thinking it. It was like falling into a hole.

She switched on the little lamp beside his bed. The fluorescent bulb blinked to life, making the room seem larger. She imagined herself getting up, putting on her coat. Pausing at the door, turning: *Do you need anything else?* Saying it even though he would not answer. And going away, down the hall lined with wheelchairs, supply cupboards. Out into the evening. There, the moon, stars. She would go in a minute. She would step into the swaying hulk of the bus, glowing with its harsh interior light. She would reach her neighbourhood, walk to her building, unlock the door of her apartment, toss her keys on the side table, stand in the hall as if something was expected, something she had momentarily forgotten. But for now, she would sit a little longer. He would stay in this bed, and a web of tubes would gradually appear over his body. Sometimes the kindly nurse would say a few words in German to him, and those words would lodge in his ear, fixing him to wherever he was. Elisabeth would sit beside him every evening, wondering if anything could have been done differently.

BLIND POET

Homer, blind poet, invoked the muses and sent Odysseus out across the wine-dark sea with grey-eyed Athena watching over him. When Odysseus made his way home to his wife, did she wish, a little, to keep on being alone because she was used to it?

Love, Sophocles wrote in a fragment from a lost play, is like a piece of ice held tight in a child's fist. You can't keep it or bring yourself to let it go. Achilles covered himself in ashes in his tent because Patroclus, whose thighs he worshipped, was dead. But ashes didn't help.

I am also blind, though not a poet. The world is an ocean of unmoored shapes and islands of isolated colour. Not born blind, though the longer I live, the less able I am to remember what it felt like to recognize objects, to move through a landscape unthinkingly. As for people, they generally irritate me—unless they stand very close they are only differently shaded variants on the same basic theme. I live alone. No white cane, no dog: I prefer to provoke annoyance instead of pity. I do collect a modest monthly disability pension, and my life is mapped as much by this as by blindness, which is a fancy way of saying I live small. I was working on a classics degree before macular degeneration arrived, fifty years too early. Someday I might go on with the degree, but for now I can't stand being read to, even by recorded voices, and I can't read to myself. *The Iliad*, let alone Simone Weil's essay on *The Iliad*, is not an easily located large-print title. Braille is vanishing, and I don't like reading on specially designed screens. I am a fairly young curmudgeon who likes books.

Sometimes I make attempts on the outside world. Don't find that pathetic. I make these attempts in an aggressive rather than a wistful spirit. One night I decided to go to an opening at the gallery below my apartment. The talk, the noise, people glancing apprehensively around a too-white room, waiting for the gallery to become the significant, elated place they hoped for. I put on a dress and sandals with small heels and earrings—round green glass beads that caught the light—glittering ragged surfaces like green suns. I probably looked beautiful, and thought, as I teetered down my steep stairs, that I would be beautiful and alone, which is very mythological.

This was an exhibit of young painters, which I found slightly poignant, since painting is about as anachronistic as Braille. Because I can only see large and bold features, the paintings looked to me (standing in the centre of the room) like disorganized gashes, disturbing the symmetry of the walls. But this was surprisingly interesting. One painting looked completely red, with darker red swirls like a cut of meat. I approached it. I put my hand on it. Textured like a cat's tongue, but stiff. Full of hills and valleys. The woman beside me hissed *What are you doing,* grabbing my arm as I tried to pull away. I knocked the glass she was holding to the floor, where it broke, and I stepped back, a curved shard stabbing in just above my arch.

Pain up my leg, shock, the air stinging the open flap of skin. Voices, then a bandage produced from somewhere, me sitting in a chair, the woman kneeling, pulling the shard quickly out of my foot.

"I am so, so, so sorry." She was drunk: her fingers frantic, her voice too precise.

"Don't worry, I'm fine, just…"

"Stay still."

"I should go home."

"No, don't, I'm sorry…look, it's my painting, I got a bit, defensive, a bit, you can't *touch* it—"

She looked at me properly. That taken aback pause.

"Sorry, are you…"

"Yup."

"I didn't realize."

"Why should you?"

I waited for the other pause, the one where I am supposed to reassure, as if the embarrassment was my problem. But instead she rose, moved away, I heard a chair being scraped across the floor, she sat down beside me, told me her name and asked me what the painting had looked like to me, what it had felt like, pressing me for details. And then she described, with unabashed egotism, what it felt like to her, as if what I most wanted to hear about in the world was her feeling. Which, in a way, right then, was true.

Her name was Marianne, after the Cohen song, she said, and I sang the opening lines. She said she was an emerging artist, would probably stay emerging till she was forty because funding was better, no one wanted to buy her paintings but that wasn't why she was a painter (her voice took on a defiant note, lying) and that she was very interested in blindness, the kind of statement that would generally make me leave immediately but this time didn't. When I finally did leave she came with me, ferrying me drunkenly upstairs, the bandage coming off my foot, the cut opening and bleeding, my sheets bloodied, and the next morning she wanted to hang it out the window like a ceremonial proof of virginity, not true in this case, and besides, I said, it was a fitted sheet, which would look stupid.

Morning. Open window. Gusts of swollen air forecasting rain. She burned food in the kitchen.

"Do you know the wiring on your toaster is fucked?"

"I can smell."

"Right. Sorry."

"Stop apologizing."

She said she wanted to make sure my foot was all right. She bleached the sheet. She made dinner, slinging plates like a line cook. After we ate she flung the dishes into the sink. One broke, but she'd stopped apologizing. She hung the bleached sheet across the window, we returned to the stripped, unfamiliar bed. Next morning the light was strained and different through the cloth.

Four days passed. The scar on my foot healed to a curved, bumpy ridge.

"Where do you *live?*"

"Do you want me to go?"

"No."

"Well then."

I didn't ask again. I don't mean I wasn't surprised or that it wasn't strange. I was afraid of her, afraid of the uncanny in her, even though it was true, I didn't want her to go. Classics scholar—I've been educated to believe in fate, not the happy resolution kind, but the older kind in which something happens to you and you bow your head and live in it, there's no other choice. She happened to me. A stranger arrives, pounds on the door or shows up at the foot of your bed; you ask them in, even if they are soaked with rain, battered by wind, dangerous, even if they are worse than dangerous. We turned on the space heaters when it got cold. We walked together in the street, I held her arm lightly, reminding her not to guide me, getting angry sometimes but the sort of anger that is established and brief, as if we knew each other well enough for that. I stopped talking to anyone else. I don't know where she lived. I don't know where she got the money to buy the groceries she hauled into the kitchen. Even now I don't know very much about her. I didn't ask. That's a recurring theme in mythology. Wait. Keep silent. Don't ask.

After a month the gallery changed its exhibit. No one bought her painting, so she moved it upstairs. It lay against a wall in the living room. I felt my way along it as I walked from the bedroom to the bathroom. I stayed out of the kitchen, because with her in it the kitchen defeated me. What had been sparsely rational became profuse. Cutlery erupted from drawers, lidless jars dotted the counter, compost containers overflowed, coffee grounds were slopped into the sink.

Cooking was colour. She made me smell before tasting, showed my fingers the specific shapes. Beets, carrots, potatoes, the obscene curve of mushrooms, a halved cabbage whorled like the maze of an open brain. She moved her work in. Canvases began to bloom along my walls.

Her hair was rough and her skin was too, especially on her hands, which were covered with calluses, raised scars, small burns. She was not clean; her armpits and head sprang with damp heavy hair. Residual traces clung to her—sweat, chemicals, paint peeling off her skin like pulled scabs. Between the cooking and the acrylic and the oil and the dirt (she liked to grind dust and hair and grime into canvases) and the sheet that stayed over the window, the apartment swam with trapped smells.

I had to ask, after a while. Because by then the thought of her leaving was too big, I couldn't imagine it. I should have known better, I should have known—never ask. The unmade bed heaped with pillows and blankets and sheets, and both of us cocooned in it and the growing lumpy disorder of the room and the question, its echoes spreading around us like the pulsing circles a stone hurled into water makes.

"How long?"

"What?"

"You won't stay, so how long?"

"Who knows."

"Will I wake up and you'll be gone?"

"Exactly."

"So long Marianne."

She didn't finish the paintings. They seemed like botched copies of the unsold red painting, which stared these down from the other side of the living room, glowering, full of authority.

"Why is it just red? Why nothing else?"

"Because," she said, sitting up in bed, naked, "I want it to look like the end of the world. I mean, why look at a painting? No one wants to buy them, why look at them? I want people to feel, looking, that something is happening. Something huge. We're so afraid that nothing will happen, that nothing will ever happen. Something has to happen. Even if it *means* the end of everything. Disaster, blood, holes in the universe, all that stuff. And then the white around the edges, the patches of white where there is no red, that's the absence, the end spaces where nothing is happening, forever. So the red is at least happening, big painful happening, it's loud and *tiring* and that's a reason to look at it. To feel something is happening."

She'd been with me long enough that the red painting had a layer of dust across the top, which furred my fingers when I brushed across it.

She'd slip out. Sometimes she left in the night. I'd wake up sprawled out, missing the cramp of making room for someone beside me.

"Are you awake?"
   "I am now."
   "It's raining out. I went out in the rain. There was a street-light. Lighting up the water. Just this glowing light, and the water, lit up."

"Come to bed."

Her feet and hands cold, her whole body alien, drawn inward.

She slept, breathing heavily, almost wheezing. The room grew light through the sheeted window.

I had softened. Become pliant, breakable. Open to different smells, to a voice, all kinds of nakedness. I put my hand up to the top of the bed frame, felt the dust along it like the dust on the painting. I didn't believe she was real, couldn't believe I'd ever thought she was real, couldn't believe I'd imagined she would stay. I must have fallen asleep at last because when I woke up it was late morning, and I was alone.

Alone sounds: the dripping tap, the hum of the space heater (it was March, wet and sunless), the rustling of wind in the trees, noise from the street. Inside the apartment an almost total silence, and me, at the centre of it, waiting. I got up, catching my foot on the painting on my way to the bathroom. I cursed, and put my hand to the frame to steady it. I sat down beside it, considering the stretch of canvas. I ran my hands over it, every bump and furrow, not caring whether my hands were clean or sweaty, not caring if I marked it. It was dry and slightly cold, the ridges of the paint reptilian under my hands, and I pressed it as if I were feeling for some kind of breath. I leaned my forehead against it and closed my eyes. Desertion demands an act of destruction and revenge, something that must be burned, an acknowledgement of betrayal and loss. Evisceration and funeral pyres. The fevered women who tore Orpheus to pieces, the rejected queen who slaughtered her own children. I thought of what was in my kitchen: knives, scissors, a kettle to boil, things that could maim. I stayed sitting on the floor, not moving, as if my perfect gesture, my way to proceed, could come to me only through the painting itself.

Theseus fell in love with Ariadne, but left her on the island of Naxos, called onwards toward his destiny. There is a vase depicting Theseus embarking on his ship while Ariadne lies sleeping. The moment when she first woke up, the other moments on that island, everything that followed, all that time after he'd gone, was she grateful to him for what she had been given? Or did she wish she'd been spared her lesson, wished she'd never seen him, wished she'd been left alone?

YOUNG HENNERLY

He watched her, wondering how long he could wait for her to speak. The lines in her face were deep, her eyes so dark he had difficulty distinguishing between iris and pupil. "Like a dried apple," but that description would have been sentimental, conveying warmth. Her hair was thin, faded to dirty white, combed back tight and pinned. Except for a belly sagging into her lap and breasts that flopped under the worn cloth of her dress, her body had shrunk around her bones. She was remarkably old. This close, her smell was very strong but not unpleasant: like burnt sugar. He thought of his grandmother in her apartment in New York, who had smelled of expensive soap, of lavender and mandarin oranges, her hands marked by ornate rings.

He looked around the room, at the linoleum floor with its deeply scored scratches, the two armchairs in front of the television, the battered coffee table with a green plastic rabbit grinning from its centre, the curtains shiny and cheap, stiff in the summer breeze. Everything was clean, as was she. The table between them looked as though it had been set up specially, in preparation for his arrival. Tea, mugs, a chipped plate with biscuits.

The room made him conscious of his fashionably thread-bare jacket, his fraying cuffs. He moved to take the jacket off, realized his shirt was soaked through with sweat, and kept it on.

"You best set that thing to go," she said at last.

He pressed the record button, listened to the familiar whir as the tape unspooled, and spoke into the microphone he'd placed between them.

"Robert Browne speaking to Mrs. Annie Reardon, August 28th, 1967, Allegheny Mountains, West Virginia. Archive of Folk Culture, Library of Congress."

Robert had avoided the Vietnam draft by means of a dissertation on American folklore coupled with a slight heart murmur, which, had he been less well-connected, might not have been enough to exempt him. Early on he'd marched in demonstrations wearing white. His friends spent their time making speeches, or chaining themselves to monuments, or going to prison, or crossing the border, vanishing. He agreed in principle, but he did not want to do anything so public and absolute. Having been excused, he resolutely buried himself in dusty libraries, in the vast records the country kept of itself.

His thesis done, he'd found work documenting American folk history. Already decades along, funded by American millionaires obsessed with the idea of the unspoiled integrity of the workingman, it was an undertaking with no end in sight. Robert liked this. There was a bracing urgency to memorialization. The work was immediate, a desperate effort to preserve each particular voice. Voices from Harlem, North Carolina, Iowa, the coast of Maine. He moved from place to place, interviewing, cataloguing, stubbornly gazing into the past.

Most people working for the Archive travelled in groups or in pairs. This had a practical dimension, since sometimes a trail took the archivists deep into backrooms, wretched tenements, bars with blackened windows, shacks in the woods. Robert preferred to work alone. That way whatever he found was his. He thought of himself as an explorer, faintly heroic. No clamorous present could compare with that mythology, in significance, in scope.

He had set out his tape recorder for Maryland oystermen, for decrepit drug-fogged musicians in Chicago, for snake-handling preachers in Wisconsin. He'd been propositioned by a tight-lipped rabbi in Brooklyn, shot at from a porch in Texas by a border patrolman who'd forgotten the scheduled interview and assumed this strange man in a car was one of many people who bore him a grudge. Truthfully, the gun had been aimed into the air, but Robert could still remember the lightness in his limbs, the tingling in his brain, as he realized the man was actually going to fire. He had talked the man down, and then conducted the interview. He thought nothing could rattle him after that.

But these people could. They told him things both true and evidently false. They sang, fiddled, and afterwards invited him to stay for dinner in their splintering houses. Their stories and songs were exactly what he wanted: old, forlorn, with a touch of horror or malice. Yet something nagged at him, some refusal or concealment lurking behind what they said. Perhaps the malice was not incidental but directed. Perhaps they took him for a fool and disliked him because, though a fool, he had driven a car down the long roads from other places and had smooth white hands.

He looked down at his hands on the table, arranged on either side of his notebook.

"Where would you like to begin, Mrs. Reardon?"

"Call me Annie, nobody says Mrs. Reardon."

"Where would you like to begin, Annie?"

"Agnes told me, Agnes Flynn, she's my sister, she says you was with her nearly two days a month ago, asking her about her cooking and when she was a girl and that, and you was always at Jim to play his fiddle. She weren't sure what it was you're set on to know."

"Anything, really. We're making an archive. Of your way of life."

He paused. He hated that phrase, the patronizing summing-up.

"Of your life, here."

What did that mean, her life here? What was here? Trees, unvarying and impenetrable. Trees, roads, more roads, roads being built, people leaving, no one arriving. Annie, in her small house. He imagined her sitting on the porch in the evenings. An authentic Appalachian scene destined to be sold as a postcard to tourists.

"I thought maybe you'd like to hear about the man who lived under the rock when I was a girl. Yes sir, that man, he lived under a *rock*."

He shifted in irritation, having heard this story many times. He wondered what the roots of it were since it occurred all over the region. Some common ancestor in England or Ireland, telling a story, embedded as local legend over time. Always presented as personal experience.

"Yes, that'd be fine to begin with."

"Well, when I was a girl, there was a man lived under a rock in the woods. He lived down a ways, and he lived under a rock, didn't have nowhere else to live, he just lived anywheres. I often think and I often study how that old man lived under that rock, how he got anything to eat. My mother said, don't go looking for that man, leave him, he got nothing to eat, he could *eat* you. He were a great tall man. He lived under that rock all weathers, down the road a ways, maybe he came out at night, when the moon was out, went hunting. That was a marvel, that man."

He wrote in his notebook: *Example of "tall tale" again: lie told with straight face.*

He kept the notebook balanced on his knee under the table, but wondered, glancing up at her, whether she could even read. A Bible sat on top of the television.

At first he'd assumed no one expected him to believe in men under rocks, or witches, or women who ate their babies. Now he was not so sure. After so many kitchen tables, so many children staring at him from front steps and backing away as he approached, so many stories told with such blind conviction, he wondered if maybe it would be easier to simply believe everything he was told, all of it.

The clock ticked. Robert sipped his tea and nibbled a biscuit, the edges crumbling at the corners of his mouth. She dipped hers in the tea, sucking it slowly through broken teeth. She began to talk more freely, running through the expected tropes, spinning them out. A man who lured girls to a shack in the woods and stewed them in a black pot and hung the heads up by the hair; a woman who murdered her sister by throwing her into a pond; a tent revival where she'd seen a woman preacher cast demons out of a young boy; a man who came home after an absence of three years and found his wife rocking a cradle with a new baby in it.

"But where was he?"

"Who?"

"The man? Where had he gone?"

"Oh, he was away to the wars, I expect."

Her eyes narrowed.

"Would you maybe like to see a picture? Of me when I was young?"

She went off into the bedroom. He rewound the tape a little and played it back.

"…and I remember when there was a revival in the tent down in the valley when I was a girl. They was women preachers in that tent, and one of them was younger and one of them was older, and they said the younger one was the old woman's girl maybe. And they was pretty good preachers, though they was women preachers. They preached about the signs and wonders. Yes sir, yes sir. Signs and wonders. How they'll be signs and wonders, when this world comes to an end. When it comes to an *end*."

He was dizzy with hunger and heat. It was late afternoon by this time, and the shadows were longer across the floor.

"Something else now we've had the tea," Annie said, returning.

She sat down, uncorking a bottle and pouring a strong alcohol into the dirty mugs. He drank quickly, his tongue stinging, his stomach in revolt. Spots of milky tea floated on the liquor.

In the photograph she offered, a young woman sat on a stool set before a cardboard sky, a child on either side. All three heads of hair were combed back harshly from stretched faces. Annie's eyes were sunken, her cheeks beginning to hollow. He could detect the shadow of the older face beneath the younger, in her eyes and the slight droop of her skin. It was impossible to tell what age she might have been in the picture. The quiet of her expression, the mixture of calm and something like rage, rendered her opaque. There was suffering in her face, and cunning, a twisting force. Malice. He pushed away the thought.

"How old would you be?" she asked. Looking up, he saw her staring at him with much the same expression as her younger self.

"Twenty-eight."

"Would've thought you'd be a soldier."

"No. I'm not."

She leaned forward over the table, putting down the mug and speaking in a whisper.

"Long time ago, long days, in the war, my grandfather said, when there was the war, the boys would hide in the woods, years and years they would hide. Sometimes they would hide in caves, or they would climb into a tree as the men passed by. Or their mothers would hide them in the floor, under the boards. They'd hide so long, moving around, you know, that when the men come and say the war was over, nobody would believe it, no sir, they just kept hiding in the woods, too scared to come out. That's how we did it then. All them boys hiding up in the trees."

He realized she must mean the Civil War, men coming along the paths, families hiding their sons in the dark woods.

"Yes sir. They *hid*. In the *trees*."

"I'm not hiding. I have—I have a heart murmur."

She leaned back, chuckling.

"Well, well, now."

She passed him the tray of biscuits. His face was still hot, and he pictured himself in her eyes, flushed, ridiculous.

"It's very different from what you think."

"Don't trouble. I know what I know. People only comes here for one reason, to hide."

"But—"

She stabbed at the picture with one forefinger.

"That one, Sam, he died at Iwo Jima. I thought, better hide him in the floor, put him in a cave somewheres, but he went and he died. They told me the sand there is black. I cried one whole year."

Her voice was flat, without a trace of self-pity or even sorrow, but she took the picture and stalked back into the bedroom angrily, as if he hadn't understood her and she didn't want him looking at it anymore.

The shame he felt was as abrupt and unmistakable as vomit in his mouth. He wanted to laugh at himself, easy, detached, but laughing made no sense. He wished that instead of a heart murmur he had some mark on his body, a sign no one would question, one leg shorter than the other, missing fingers. He stood, and found his hands were shaking.

It was nearly dark. August was like that, creeping up, and the nights here were cold. He thought about the drive back, the steep turns of the road. He had driven these roads at night but could never shake the fear of becoming lost, his headlights shining ineffectually only a few feet into the trees, and beyond that, complete blackness. Looking down, he saw he'd emptied the mug.

From outside he heard crickets, leaves rustling, a twig breaking somewhere, the squeaking of bats.

Her voice sounded from the bedroom, a low-pitched rumble followed by higher notes, a breathy wheezing. She was singing, slowly attempting to remember a song, as softly as she could. It sounded like an incantation though he could not make out any words. He thought, with drunken lucidity, that she was a witch. Or more than that, worse than that, that she was the wood, an inhuman voice from the trees. These people believed in the horror of the wild—that something watched among the leaves, crafty, waiting. Malice. He didn't want to believe this himself, but only to preserve the belief. He had been taught that if one behaved well, one would be rewarded, and in his case, what he had been taught was true. He had been excused, and the worst things, the unthinkable things, had passed him by while grasping others: the young men who hid in trees, in cellars, under floors. The black sand.

He should leave. It was dark on the road. He did not want to look at her face anymore. He gathered up his notebook, his bag. As he buttoned up his jacket, he knocked the biscuit plate onto the floor. It did not break, and as he bent to pick it up he heard her re-enter the room.

"I will sing you 'Young Hennerly,' and then you will go."

She tipped the last of the bottle into her mug and carefully screwed the cap back on. Not knowing what else to do, he sat.

Her hair was down now. She looked like a figure carved from wood. She grinned, her lips smacking wetly as she set the mug back down on the table.

"This is a song I knew a long time ago."

Leaning back in her chair, her hand stroking the surface of the table, she began to sing.

Come in, come down, Young Hennerly
And stay all night with me.
The very best lodging that I can afford
Will be much better for thee.
I can't come down, I won't come down
And stay all night with you.
For I've a girl in the merry green land,
I love her much better than you.

Her voice cracked on the high notes, growled on the low ones. The song was slow, mournful, and her singing made him think of a door blowing in the wind, the grinding of rusted hinges, metal against metal.

She leant herself against the fence
And kisses gave him three.
The girl you love in the merry green land,

She ain't no better than me.
She took him by the lily-white hand,
The other by the feet;
She plunged him into the deep blue well
That was more than a hundred feet.

Her hand slowly moved toward him over the table. She kept a kind of stroking rhythm, advancing and retreating, but each time her hand came further forward. He wondered what would happen if she touched him.

Lie there, lie there, Young Hennerly,
Till the flesh rots off your bones;
That girl you love in the merry green land
Will be waiting for your return.
Fly down, fly down, you pretty parrot bird,
And set on my right knee;
Your cage shall be out of the best of gold
And your doors out of ivory.

He wanted to take notes or at least shift a little away from her, but his head spun and he could not move.

I won't fly down, I shan't fly down,
Nor stay all night with you,
For a girl that'll murder her own true love
Will murder a bird like me.

She stopped, drew back her hand. He pushed back his chair.

"Well. Thank you very much, Annie."

"Yes, so."

He waited. She did not get up.

"Should I see myself out?"

"If you like. But it's a big night outside. Careful on the road."

He went, leaving her sitting at the table, the empty mug in front of her, and the plate of sugary crumbs.

Outside, he set each foot down delicately on the wooden steps and found his way to his car. A bat swooped low just over his head.

He sat in the car, sweating, almost in tears. She was standing in the open doorway, her hair hanging around her shoulders against the cloth of her now nearly transparent dress, the light shining through to the bare suggestion of sinew and bone.

The motor, roaring into life, reassured him. He felt the weight of his foot on the gas, his hands on the steering wheel as he turned out of her yard and onto the road. He would drive through the night, back down the side of the mountain and to his motel where he would eat a sandwich and write some notes. He would hang a fresh shirt out for the morning, line his shoes neatly beside each other, read a little and go to bed, the bleached sheets holding him, his clothes folded on the chair.

He turned a corner past a huge rock and his headlights caught the shape of a tall man, who swung out suddenly to the road, his arms raised as if he was preaching or asking for help. Robert slammed on the brakes, throwing up a cloud of dust. The man blinked and lowered his arms, standing so close he was almost touching the hood, staring into Robert's face through the windshield, waiting to see what Robert would do. His eyes, catching the light, were very pale, and his hair was greasy around his shoulders. Robert sat, his heart thudding, and then, recklessly trying to prove himself to himself, he leaned over and opened the passenger door.

"Need a lift?"

The man nodded and got in without speaking. His skin shone as though he was sweating. He leaned back into the seat, smiling to himself.

"Just for a couple of miles," the man said, and his voice was ragged, as if he hadn't spoken for a long time. His clothes were dirty, but recognizable as the clothes of an ordinary man, aside from the height and the pallid shining skin. He's a hitchhiker, Robert told himself, just a regular hitchhiker. They drove on in silence, the man beginning to doze.

SONG AND DANCE

Today was her Song and Dance. Gillian would stand in front of the class sitting in their half-circle on metal chairs with the black plastic seats covered in hard bumps like an ossified tongue, and she would recite a nursery rhyme. *Recite* was a misnomer: she would moan and flail and squirm, with luck she would cry, she'd seen other people cry, sensed the silent respect and jealousy of the room, and Helen's approval. Gillian wanted tears, grey welts on her powdered cheeks.

Gillian stood, did a few shoulder rolls, walked under the line of track lights at the far end (the other lights were switched off for this part of the class, the covered video cameras and furniture and surplus chairs looming in the half-dark behind the faces). She was still dressed for her Scene Study, where she played a sex worker who the man in the scene called a whore, but nobody said *sex worker* yet, not even butch Kim, who whistled when Gillian came out of the dressing room in her tights and black slip and shiny red Goodwill heels. Later Gillian knew to say *sex worker* and dislike whistling, but today, seventeen and unfamiliar with herself, it made her feel transformed, not a shy girl who wanted to be an actor and wore embroidered blouses and had never had a boyfriend let alone a girlfriend. She was someone Kim would whistle at.

Everyone in the class wanted to be an actor except Helen, who was. The stuffy room was a multi-use studio on Richmond, carpeted in red with darker swirls like a cut of meat, gummed here and there with indeterminate black stains. Wednesdays they did Scene Study and Song and Dance; Saturdays were On Camera. Gillian could hear an ambulance passing down in the street.

She was under the lights now.

"Take off your shoes, please," Helen said.

Helen sat very straight, independent of the chair back. She wore a blue scarf the same colour as her eyes, a long black dress, black sandals that laced up over her calves. Her hair was so white it glowed.

When Gillian didn't move quickly enough, Helen knelt, took Gillian's foot in her hands and slid off her shoe. Gillian was afraid her toes smelled, grubby in the fishnets. She didn't know what to do: should she take off the other shoe herself, or present her right foot to Helen? Removing her own shoe might look like refusing an offer, and you must never, never, never, Helen told them, refuse an offer, which was why when Gillian's scene partner Mitch pulled her hair and spat in her face she did not object. It would be wrong to block his impulses. Mitch was a small cheerful roosterish man who was training as a paramedic but in the scene he'd managed to summon a whiff of persuasive masculine violence, unmistak-able as a match flaring. He grabbed her wrist and twisted. After, they were both wrung out and queasy and pleased.

Gillian offered her other foot.

Helen took the shoes and returned to her seat, placing the heels beside her.

"When you're ready," she said.

Gillian did not begin yet. She'd seen enough of these to know that you did not begin right away, not until you felt the impulse. It had to be the real impulse, the truthful one. Helen would know if it wasn't. You stood, and you were looked at. Everyone looked. You breathed and allowed your-self to be vulnerable, and you were looked at. She'd seen others be vulnerable, immediate, authentic in their Song and Dance, and she wanted to be more vulnerable, more authentic, more immediate, but she knew you couldn't plan that, that was the point, you were learning to just be, in the primal place, the gut place. You had to learn to be, though Gillian didn't know exactly what. More, Helen said often, you must be more, just more, more, and more, she said, and brought her palms together gently and let her hands fall into her lap and fixed them with her blue gaze and her sharply cut hair fell forward along her cheeks.

Gillian breathed. Flexed the balls of her feet.

"Feel when you are ready," Helen said. "Stretch out."

Gillian stretched out her arms like she was going to catch an enormous ball, a ball larger than her body. She would be more than herself. She had chosen her nursery rhyme weeks before. She would sing it, howl it, march in a circle, dance like a piece of knotted rag jerked on a string, she would get her tears and be amazed by them, her hands fluttering like aspen leaves. She would not, as Helen kept reminding them, attempt to find meaning in the words. The point of Song and Dance was to have no meaning or control, only impulse. To use the text as a vessel that was capacious and neutral, blanched of significance, able to hold anything you put into it. To express that you were present and free. Gillian would prove herself today. Helen would tell her she was free.

Beyond the lights, faces. Kim, scrubbed and earnest, legs apart. Jennifer, made up in pale pinks and mauves, who already had an agent who got her work as a stand-in on the sets of American films that shot in Toronto. She'd once stood in for Holly Hunter because they were the same size. Holly Hunter was really nice and asked her about places to eat downtown near her hotel but Jennifer didn't know; she lived in North York and only came downtown (driving, she was afraid of the subway) for this class. Joanie, who was the oldest, as old as Helen herself, and worked as a receptionist and went to open auditions and appeared in community theatre productions of Tennessee Williams and once a play by T. S. Eliot where she was in the chorus (Gillian had gone to see her, sitting on a folding chair in the tiny theatre in the basement of a mall). Joanie had inhaled loudly before every line, as if to prepare the audience. She sat now with her arms crossed, dyed red hair tightly coiled, eyebrows plucked and redrawn in black pencil, her face staunchly melancholy like a bullfrog. Mitch, flushed from the success of their Scene Study. There was a fleck of spit in one corner of his mouth. Michelle, pretty, frighteningly thin, skin spattered with uneven freckles, one eyelid twitching behind frameless glasses. She wept steadily through the relaxation exercises that began each class, while Helen walked between their prone bodies, and they lay on the floor with the lights off and tried to intuit their breathing, Michelle's sobs audible over the synthesized music Helen played. Michelle had been Gillian's scene partner in the previous unit, and they'd met to rehearse in Michelle's basement apartment, mostly sitting drinking coffee while Michelle talked about her boyfriend, who was twice her age (she was twenty-four) and paid for the apartment, and Gillian felt chastened by her own inexperience.

Michelle glowered in her chair. She took off her glasses, rubbed the twitching lid. That was the whole of the class. A select group, Helen said. Helen sat in the centre of the row.

Helen was from New York and had moved to Toronto fifteen years earlier. She took on small numbers of students for her acting classes, offered in this tired building. Gillian had been required to meet with her, in a coffee shop near the studio, in order to be vetted for the class. She was the youngest one there and paid for the classes by babysitting. Helen had told Gillian that her teaching methods were strongly Meisner-influenced, that she would expect each student to get out of their comfort zone, to be willing to take risks for artistic truth. Gillian left the coffee shop longing to be allowed into this club of people who were braver and freer than other people.

For the first class she arrived early and sat in the hall. Helen arrived late, unbuttoning her coat as she walked into the room, already talking, dropping the coat on the floor. Gillian studied the faces of her classmates, wondering what special thing Helen had seen in them. Helen had seen something in her. She wanted to pick up Helen's coat but didn't.

In retrospect Gillian knew that none of them was special, they were just the few people foolish enough to pay a woman with a couple of acting credits from the seventies and eighties to tell them who they ought to be. Helen had seemed old to Gillian, with her smoker's whisper that you strained to catch, the white blades of her hair. Her silk scarves undulated around her neck and her hands reached at the air, moulding it as she spoke. She told stories about touring in a new Mamet play, about playing Irina in *Three Sisters*, about meeting John Huston at a party when he was a very old man. None of her stories concerned her present, as if she had ceased to have a private life and existed only for her students, an icon they could pray to, kept in a cupboard when not in use.

When Helen died of lung cancer and Gillian's mother sent her the small obituary, Gillian found she'd been married, had a son, a few minor film roles (there was no mention of theatre work), and would have been in her late forties when Gillian knew her. Those twice-weekly acting classes from the two years when Gillian was going to be an actor must have been only the tiniest part of Helen's life, something that would allow her the centrality that marriage and children would not permit. Helen, throned in her chair, testing them to see if they were worthy. Song and Dance was the biggest test.

"You are not in your body yet," Helen said mildly, and got up, testing her weight on each foot, putting her hands on Gillian to adjust her. Waist, hips, sternum. Warm indifferent hands, palm solidly placed.

"Send your breath into my hand," she said.

Gillian concentrated, thinking of her breath as a creature that was seeking Helen's hand. Something independent of her mind, something prior to her mind, that was what Helen wanted her to understand, that there was something in her to be released, something more important than her will, something she did not choose. She was not supposed to choose. Helen took her hands away and went swiftly back to her chair, and Gillian knew she had failed. She was still thinking, still trying to choose.

Helen had told them the story of studying with Sanford Meisner in New York. He had put his hand up her skirt in front of the class. Not salaciously, Helen said, but to provoke a reaction, to teach her to break away from learned behaviors that prevented her from responding instinctively. Her bodily response was deeper than her thinking. Confusion, shame: these things made her vulnerable, and her vulnerability was her gift. Helen told them, her voice even lower than usual, that this was the greatest lesson she'd ever received. She hadn't known where to look. Blood had flooded her face. She had cried.

There, he said, *that's it. That's right.* She understood.

It was her turning point, Helen said. Gillian wanted a turning point.

Gillian, sitting at her laptop late at night with her child asleep behind her, looked up Sanford Meisner. Black-and-white photo of a man in heavy glasses, his thick hair sculpturally mounted on his head, his eyes sliding off to one side, an expression of amused authority. Helen was dead, and Gillian knew when she had been born and that she would have been a very young woman when Meisner taught her, a child compared to him. Gillian examined the bony large hand with which he held his chin, thought of the motion of thrusting up a skirt, imagined a clinical appraisal as Helen blushed and wept, looking around for help and seeing from the faces of her classmates that this was expected.

Gillian didn't feel angry on Helen's behalf. At that point in her life she was tired of anger; it had come to seem like a stock response. Instead she was baffled by the man's naïveté, that he would think he could give this young woman what he judged was freedom, that he would not realize she was still calculating, trying to gauge what he wanted, offering him what he wanted. What conceit, believing he could discover her that easily, that she had no designs of her own. A stupid man, thinking his students had true selves that could be revealed by a pinch or grab. Helen, wet-eyed, red-faced, absorbing a different lesson. His complacent kingliness, his nod to the room. He showed her what she wanted to be.

There. That's it. That's right.

Gillian raises her daughter alone, is preoccupied by bills and worry, worry, worry, worry. She sometimes wishes she had agreed to marry her girlfriend when she was asked to, because then perhaps she wouldn't have been so easily left, shrugged off along with their child like an outgrown coat, like Helen's coat dropped on the floor. Gillian, as usual, has been drawn to power, to smirk and swagger. She's been duped. That is why she thinks of Helen, awake late at night thinking of her own delusions of freedom as a tangible thing that, when attained, would open her up to her real life. Still withheld, deferred, something she is on the verge of but has not yet reached, not there yet, never quite there. She doesn't believe anymore in that arrival but she still longs for it, late at night with her daughter asleep, catches herself thinking that there should be more. Wasn't there more? More what? Just more. Wasn't there? No, of course not, she tells herself, staring at the screen, that was only what you thought when you were seventeen and wanted to be an actor.

Sing a song of sixpence
A pocket full of rye

Four and twenty blackbirds
Baked in a pie
When the pie was opened
The birds began to sing
Wasn't that a dainty dish—

And Helen nodded.

BOYS

He was a small boy, younger than me. His ribs stuck out, his hands weren't strong. When he gripped my arm, it was a timid squeeze. His hair fanned out, greenish under the water, like he was already drowned. When I let go he came up crying, then snot and tears came running down his face, his eyes astounded. But he didn't tell anyone. I knew he wouldn't. I knew it was something he'd let me get away with.

We were both named James. It was our grandfather's name, and I got it first. But when James was born, his mother died, and when my uncle declared he would call the baby James, my parents thought it wasn't the right moment to object. When we got older, everyone called me Jimmy, then Jim. He stayed James.

He was slow. He faltered sometimes with words, and other times they bubbled out of him. He said things that couldn't possibly be true. Nothing would stop him. His soft hair stuck up around his head, fine as baby hair, he wore thick glasses that slipped down his nose. The corners of his mouth were damp. He was always wiping his mouth on his sleeve.

"Why don't you go see James?" My mother would say this—a refrain—as if she'd just thought of it, as if I had a choice. I dropped my school knapsack down and walked the three blocks to my uncle's house, kicking the pavement to scuff up my new shoes.

We would walk together along the main drag, James stumping along happily like we were friends, and I let him think that, even though I was forced out the door by my mother's indignation at my uncle's failures. "Blind as a bat!" she would say to my father. "Pretending everything will be fine. But it won't! It's not fair, treating James as if he didn't need any help!"

We'd walk until the road widened. We'd squat down in the long grass beside the paved shoulder of the highway, scrabble together a pile of stones. This was his favourite game—trying to hit the trucks as they went by, listening for the ping of the rock striking the metal as they roared up and over the hill, gone.

"I got one! I got one! Did you hear?"

"Yeah. Maybe I heard that one."

"You know what?" he yelled, one hand wiping across his chin.

"What?"

"I'm gonna drive a truck!"

"That's great."

"Really really. Eighteen-wheeler."

"You'd get tired. Truckers have to drive like fourteen hours a day."

"No I'll never get tired, I'll drink coffee and I'll smoke cigarettes and listen to the radio, I'll never get tired."

He sucked back air, and I swatted at bugs, the day hot and buzzing. I felt cramped whenever we were together, because I was twelve and ached from growing. We waited for the next truck. None came.

"I'm bored."

"Me too," James said proudly, as if we'd achieved something. We walked down to the creek, which had very clear water. Chemical runoff from the factory had killed the murky creek life. A snake slithered through the brown grass, right by our feet, and James jumped.

"It's gonna bite me!"

"It's a grass snake, stupid, a garter, it won't bite anybody."

We watched the snake.

"Want me to kill it?"

"Can you?"

I stomped on the snake's head. The body twitched once and the blood sprang out, mixing with brains and muscle under my shoe. I felt like a general, brilliant and brutal, with my wet-mouthed army of one. James squealed, jumping up and down, flapping his hands in the air.

"Do it again!"

We ran around on the grass and through the bushes near the water, searching, and finally found another snake, smaller than the first one.

"Can you do it again?"

"You can do this one, if you want."

He looked at it.

"No. You."

I raised my foot, higher this time, watching James. We were both grinning like maniacs, and it was a good day suddenly, the hot light of late summer flashing around us, and I was a person of substance, reflected in James's eyes.

The snake burst over our shoes, and we washed them off in the creek.

We walked home together, swinging our arms, James a little off balance, trying to imitate me and throwing his weight too far forward like a wounded man compensating for a limp.

My uncle was waiting for us on the front porch, smiling anxiously. He was always a little anxious: his expensive suits didn't fit him well, his ties were too loud, his pants too short, his collar not straight, or poking up at the back. He was the richest man I knew, and though he was a lawyer his real money came from James's mother. Serious money, my mother said, and I pictured it laid out in solemn rows. Money that came from a long way back, sawmills or railroads or something, setting him above everyone else in town, and far above my parents. He tried to be a rich man and pretended that James would grow up to be an ordinary rich boy who wore a blazer and white shirt, a boarding school student on the outskirts of a more picturesque town who would some day become a lawyer himself.

I watched James amble up the steps.

My uncle bought a cottage on Lake Joe shortly after James was born. The cottage didn't fit him any better than his suits, and he roamed across it aimlessly, wishing he were at work. But it must have seemed like a necessary part of establishing what he hoped for. We went there every summer, my mother cooking and cleaning and James and me living in the water, wrinkled and burnt. Or we tramped through the scrub trying to figure out a game, the hemlock trees and moss not quite concealing how civilized it all was, a vista of neighbours and boats. We left stashes of food and unfinished tree houses and dugouts all over the place, until the property took the form of my limited imagination and James's willingness to do anything I asked.

One weekend a woman arrived. My uncle had been making trips to Toronto for months, leaving James with us, but he'd said nothing and hadn't even told us that there would be a visitor until she pulled into the driveway, calling out as she opened the car door.

"So this is where you've been hiding!" My uncle kissed her cheek. My mother came out of the house and down the steps.

"This is Lori."

He smiled to himself as he carried her bags into the house.

Lori exclaimed over the view, the rocks and trees, the screened-in porch, the exposed beams, the fireplace. He followed her around, dazzled, perhaps amazed that this polished woman was willing to take him on. James was silent. I was fascinated by the texture of her tanned body, smoothly uniform like a leather purse, revealed in a pink bikini, and the sweep of her dyed reddish brown hair over her shoulders. Beside her, my mother looked pale and lumpy as a plucked chicken.

My mother sat in a deck chair reading a book while Lori talked about her work in Toronto, and smiled on my uncle, at the water and the boathouse and James and I splashing each other in the shallows, just out of earshot. Lori had plans; my mother was sure of it.

"We're moving to Toronto," James announced. We were standing in the water, trying to skip stones.

"No you aren't, stupid."

"Yeah. My dad said."

"Why?"

"Lori has a house she likes. So we're gonna move there."

"Do you want to?"

"Maybe you can come with me?"

"I don't want to come with you, stupid."

He punched me on the shoulder, hurt, and I punched him back, laughing, the two of us struggling, splashing, the water closing over his head, my hands pressing down on his hair.

They moved away the next spring. We stood in the driveway of their sold house and waved, as my uncle scolded James into his seat, buckling the belt for him as if he might try to jump out of the car. Lori waited for them in Toronto, ready in her better house.

James leaned out the window, yelling. "Bye! Bye!"

My mother placed one hand on my shoulder. "Well. No one can say I didn't try."

I shrugged her off. As the car disappeared over the hill, I shook myself free of James, of his increasingly useless love.

I walked. Walking felt better than the rush of buses and subways, and I didn't have a car. I'd scribbled the address on a scrap of paper, softening in my damp hand. It was getting dark as I walked along Sherbourne past the wasteland of high-rises and rooming houses and Christian missions for men with bloodshot eyes and halting walks, whose wives would never take them back. Past Moss Park with its big trees and playground equipment covered in graffiti. Cabbagetown was a shock—I wasn't familiar with the crossovers of cities, how one class and status gives way to another without warning. When I found the right street I was engulfed by an eerie silence, broken by the whoosh of cars and the footfalls of well-dressed women walking their small dogs.

I was twenty, not interested in school, sick of my mother, and hoping to find some kind of work in Toronto. I'd saved enough money from a summer construction job to cover a few months' rent on a basement bachelor apartment. I walked around the city, looking in windows, sure my solitary anonymity wouldn't last, sure it must be something unpleasant but temporary, like a flu. I sometimes noticed my own reflection, my badly fitting clothes, my ingratiating angry face, but only in passing, as if I would shed all that shortly for something else. I was happy to be invited to dinner. Maybe I missed James a little, or missed the way he made me feel—like everything I did had a witness.

The house was tall and narrow behind a wrought iron gate. Lori answered the door. She kissed my cheek, her mouth dry against my skin. Pot lights overhead cast long shadows on the hardened planes of her face. My uncle trailed behind her, meek, balding. Behind him came James.

He was heavier, as tall as me. He had a better pair of glasses, but his face was blandly childish even at nineteen. He came forward and hugged me, holding me lightly as if afraid he might crease my shirt.

"James," Lori said warningly, and my uncle made a face behind her, a violent involuntary face. But when we all sat down to dinner he took her hand, holding it as we clinked our glasses.

"To the boys," he said.

"James is working in a law office," Lori said, running her finger along the stem of her glass, smiling reprovingly at my uncle, who'd just picked a green tendril of salad from his front teeth.

"His mother's cousin is a partner there," my uncle added, rolling the green stem into a ball between his thumb and finger.

"But James is doing very well."

James blinked and nodded.

"I'm sure they find James helpful," she went on. I'd forgotten how she spoke to James, her voice wheedling, as if he was withholding something she wanted. How she looked beyond his shoulder when he answered her.

I watched James holding his fork in a clenched fist, and tried to imagine him in some Toronto office, wondering what they found for him to do. Maybe he sorted through files, ran errands. I pictured him sitting at a desk, staring longingly at the road, at the passing cars.

After dinner I helped Lori with the dishes, loading the dishwasher clumsily as she soaped the pots. James and his father went out on the patio together and lit cigarettes. I could see them through the window, shoulders braced in the cold, contentedly puffing. She pointed out her garden, snowed-under mounds and furrows that meant flowers and bushes.

"In the summer, you must come back and see it."

"That would be great."

A pause, the clatter of pots placed on the draining board.

"We have something we want to ask you."

I waited; she kept her eyes on the pan in her soapy hands.

"We need some help with James. Do you know what I mean?"

James could dress himself, talk, he could drive a car, he could read, follow directions to a destination, hold a fork. He'd never needed help except with his unacknowledged loneliness and a wish to be someplace else. They could buy him a truck, I thought. That would help. But she went on before I could answer, and I saw that an answer wasn't expected.

"He needs someone to watch him, to—to keep an eye on him. Someone who can be trusted."

"Trusted how?"

She handed me a towel.

"There have been some misunderstandings lately. Some inappropriate friendships. With boys. Nothing serious."

"Serious?"

She smiled tightly.

"We need someone we can call, who can keep an eye on him. Who can deal with people. His father finds it difficult."

"What, like, follow him around?"

She didn't answer, instead bent down to shut the door of the dishwasher, taking the towel from me and slowly drying her hands, looking at me for the first time.

"Someone who can watch him when he needs to be watched. We would appreciate this very much, and we'll show it, now and in the long term. We really appreciate your help."

She touched my arm with the towel.

"It will be a big help," she repeated. She opened the patio door. "Come in, sinners! You'll both freeze! James, *please* take your boots off on the mat."

When I got home that night I found three hundred dollars in the pocket of my coat and a note from my uncle.

More as needed.

This was how it went: phoned and instructed by Lori, I would follow James to the park and stand behind the bushes, looking like a man to be avoided, not a protective observer. This began in the late fall, when the nights were cold. James walked to the park nearly every evening. He sat down on a bench, his coat in folds around him. He tried to strike up conversations with bored or lonely boys who hung out near the playground, as unsure as he was about a place to go or anything to do. Not young children exactly—thirteen or fourteen years old—killing time before adulthood swallowed them up. If he were lucky a boy would sit beside him for a while, embarrassed by the oddball young man, but interested too. James listened. He bought things—food, cigarettes. He had a wallet full of cash, and he was kind, and besides, these boys were fragile, the timid ones, not welcome in the groups that hung out in the schoolyard after dark. I couldn't get near enough to hear their exchange of words.

I was lost in the city, in the aggrieved crowds, and I had no work. I looked at the faces of rooming-house men, almost my own face, or what my face might become. Money is money. I didn't know what else to do. So I watched.

When James was lucky, a boy would come back, the meeting prearranged, and would be invited into James's blue BMW, a present from his father. James was a good driver, and his pride matched his skill. I stayed behind, watching them go. I didn't know where they drove. I didn't know what they talked about.

Every few months there was a new favourite boy to take for drives. One boy would get tired of it. Or maybe something would happen, a small gesture or request. What was it? A hand reached out, a fumbled moment? I never found out. It didn't seem as if James minded the change very much, as long as there was someone beside him, a face to look at sidelong as he drove, a face taut and delicate in the light of the street lamps.

I wasn't invited to dinner again. Just phone calls, followed by cheques. Lori made the calls, my uncle signed the cheques, though what he thought he was doing, I don't know. I'm not foolish. I know the words that might have been said of James. Hunter, predator, keeping an eye out for boys who had fallen behind, who were without armour, who came from the high-rises where the lobbies smelled like piss and the elevators clanked and groaned, whose parents were preoccupied, defeated. I knew the words and I didn't try to stop him. I thought of him as a child. I still believe, mostly, that he was harmless. Grinning, trusting, watching me kill snakes beside the creek. It's impossible to get that image of him to resolve into something calculating and sinister. Even as I watched him open the car door with bumbling courtesy, watched the car turn the corner out of sight, I believed in his innocence. I don't know if I was wrong.

Months passed. A year. Then amazingly, two. I kept the apartment. I cashed the cheques. I got a part-time job shelving books in a library, which didn't pay enough to cover my rent but gave me a way to pretend I wasn't living off dubious family arrangements. One day, for the first time, the cheque was unexpectedly large, with a note attached, from Lori, the new urgency apparently too distasteful to convey over the phone. I was asked to talk to someone. A mother.

I put on a suit. I bought it at the Goodwill, but it fit me well, didn't bunch up or hang too loose. Charcoal grey. I thought I ought to look like a different kind of man, imposing and capable. The other man, for whom nothing worked out, who had an unnecessarily large vocabulary, who might never be able to find anywhere to fit, was temporarily absent.

The mother's name was Shelley, and she'd followed James home, yelled from the porch, been promised a meeting in a place she chose, Lori speaking to her through the closed screen door. She got up when I arrived in the lobby of her building, pulling at the edge of her purple shirt, one of those vaguely medieval hippie shirts with swooping sleeves. I'd imagined a young woman, young enough to be mistaken for her child's sister, but Shelley's face was lined, her voice deep. She had very bright green eyes that were a little bloodshot, and she grasped my hand hard when I offered it, though her grip was shaky. Red and blue bead earrings hung to her shoulders, clashing with the shirt, and I pictured her dressing carefully in the same spirit as I'd chosen the suit. Hoping for a different, luckier person.

"You his cousin?"

"Jim. Pleased to meet you."

We sat on a bench beside a fake fern. She pressed her hands down on either side of her, her fingers working over a burn hole on the vinyl upholstery.

"I don't want to cause trouble. It's just…"

"You're concerned. Anyone would be."

"Yeah. Leo's friendly, he wants friends, it's just…I don't want him getting into a car. I mean, who thinks it's okay to take a boy into his *car*—do you think it's okay?"

I waited, wondering how much she would let herself say.

"I don't know what I should do."

I was surprised by how easy she was making it for me. When I looked at her she looked away, already losing ground. I realized that I made her afraid, and I couldn't help enjoying the feeling, it was so unfamiliar.

"You know, Shelley, James isn't going to hurt anybody. He's just friendly."

"Friendly."

"He doesn't understand how it might look."

"What if I call the police?"

"I wouldn't do that."

She dug her finger into the burn hole, pulling out a strand of yellowed stuffing.

"Why not?"

"What would you tell them? What could you actually tell them?"

"But I want—I want…"

"Anyone would want to protect their son, wouldn't they? But has he said he's been—"

"No. No, he didn't *say*…"

"Then what would *you* say?"

"I'm not stupid."

"Of course not."

"I'm not stupid."

"I think James is easy to misunderstand."

She nodded, not agreeing, not seeing what else to do. I told her about James, told her about when we were kids, James yearning for company. I told her that my uncle was a lawyer, and I managed to work that in casually, as if it wasn't important, and later, just as casually, I offered her an envelope. She took it without looking inside, and I left wondering if we had both expected this from the moment we shook hands or if I had surprised her, if she would despise herself, shaking the money out onto the counter after the ride in the elevator, after locking the door of her apartment, if her son would come home and find her sitting on the couch, wondering what deal she had struck.

Complaints didn't happen very often. I kept some of my uncle's money in reserve; sometimes I didn't even have to use it. I didn't intentionally frighten the mothers, or not much. And when I did use the money, I imagined they were reluctantly glad to have it. Like I was.

My uncle died one Sunday at the end of summer. Lori told me he had been reading the paper on the couch. James had been mowing the front lawn. Lori was in the backyard, tying up a row of sunflowers. If he cried out no one heard him over the noise of the mower. He was lying on the floor when James found him, one hand reaching over his head. It had been a quick death.

I sat beside James at the funeral, Lori on the other side. My mother, crammed in beside Lori, had saved a space for me beside her. I could feel her offence, tamped down, as she whispered across James, "Good for you, Jim. You take care of him," as if James couldn't hear. He stared straight ahead, sucking ponderously on his bottom lip. Lori glanced at him from time to time during the service, her hand reaching toward his face as though she wanted to wipe his nose, which for once didn't need wiping. We sang a few desultory hymns. When we stood up to leave I put my hand on James's arm and he grinned at me, showing teeth, as if we two, stuck together, were all he needed.

Lori came to see me. She stood in my apartment vibrating with energy and couldn't bring herself to sit. Towels hung damp over the backs of chairs, plates caked with food filled the sink, a small dead plant sat in the centre of the table.

"I'm selling the house."

"Oh."

"That might seem shocking."

"Well—"

"It's been a lot of responsibility for me. I want something smaller, more manageable. I know this is a lot to ask of you."

"What are you asking?"

"You've been so understanding. And James is family. His father cared about family so much."

I shrugged, trying to make her as uncomfortable as I could. But I didn't really blame her. She wanted to own a condo and play tennis and go for walks to little cafés and join a book club and be happy. She was obstinately good at being happy.

"I can't be expected to look after him forever, can I?" she nearly whimpered, suddenly unguarded and old. It might have been a ploy, but I knew I'd still say yes to what she asked. Yes. I will. Yes.

She left James to me. She moved to St. Catharines and called me once a week. She helped me to arrange the money his father had left him, enough to last him several lifetimes. She arranged money for me. She drove away.

"Do you like it?"

We stood in the living room of a low-rise apartment I'd found for him, close to where he'd lived. James looked around, overwhelmed by the three rooms and white electric stove, the squares of tile in the kitchenette, the gleaming tub.

"Can I live here?"

"If you want."

"But I'll have to clean it."

I laughed. "I'll help you."

He nodded, looking up as if we were in a cathedral.

"Yeah. I like it. It's great."

"How much help will he need?" The super, Rita, watched James going from room to room, running his hands along the windowsills, opening the fridge door.

"He'll be fine. If he makes trouble, you can call me."

"I don't want trouble."

"Okay. There won't be any."

She jangled the keys in one hand, considering.

"As long as he's quiet," she said finally. "This is a quiet building."

The hallways were drab, the paint chipped, the building sliding slowly toward the time when it would be torn down or become a rooming house for men who were like James in every way except that they had no money. The people who lived in it now worked in offices, most of them single, their lives there temporary. I thought the shabbiness would suit him, and as he stood on the brown broadloom and looked out the window, he appeared satisfied.

"He's quiet," I said to Rita. Her flowered dress smelled of chemical roses and tobacco, her hair was vibrantly gold with grey at the roots, and I could tell from the way she stood that her feet hurt her. This moved me unexpectedly, making me wonder about my mother's feet.

"I live in the basement with my grandson. I don't mind keeping an eye."

We moved him in. I took him shopping, helped him learn to cook as much as he needed to. Noodles, things poured from cans, or already prepared, covered in plastic and tinfoil. He learned to clean, wiping and sweeping with immense concentration, his tongue sticking out slightly, his head bent to the floor. He joyously quit his job, and we bought him new clothes. Jogging pants, sweatshirts, T-shirts. The button-downs and creased tan pants Lori had bought for him were stuffed into a garbage bag. He invited me over for dinner and served me soup and crackers and cheese, bringing the food to the little table, making me sit while he washed the dishes, soaping each one individually, testing the heat of the water, drying each thing and putting it away. He shuffled, he wiped his mouth on his sleeve, his glasses were crooked, but in his own place, with his own things, he looked less like a child and more like a shy, unprepossessing man. He was happy. I thought I had done that.

I ran into Rita in the hall. A boy slouched behind her.

"Hey Jim. This is my grandson, Mike."

She clutched his shoulder.

"Say hello, Mike."

He licked his lips. He was small, I guessed ten or eleven, and his hair was mousy, colourless, stiffened like straw around his face. His eyes were a little sunken, with raised violet pouches underneath, and his freckled skin had the sallow look of someone who spends his days in classrooms and his nights playing video games, someone who lives off french fries and Coke.

"No manners?" she laughed, her hand tightening.

"Is James any trouble?" I asked, smiling at Mike, who looked away.

"No, no, he's fine, we like him fine, don't we? He's friendly. We have a smoke sometimes, out on the deck. Some of the other ones, they're snooty, but James is a nice man."

When the phone rang I was climbing out of the shower and I let it ring for a while, expecting Lori's weekly call. I would tell her about dinner. I might even tell her we'd thrown out the clothes. I stood on the carpet, water dripping at my feet.

"Is this Jim?"

"Yes?"

"You said I could call. You gave me the number. It's Rita. I don't want to bother you."

I could hear her pull on her cigarette.

"I went to the store, right? I just got back. Mike's gone."

"Gone?"

"Well, Mike is old enough to come and go, but then there was a message, I must've missed it, this message from James."

"What did he say?"

"I *said*, I *always* said to Mike, don't bother James, you leave him, but James likes to have him over, did you know?"

"I—"

"Doesn't bother me. I like James fine. He's quiet. Like you said."

"Where is James?"

"So he said on the message they went somewhere, he took Mike somewhere, to this place he has, he said they'd be back in a few days, not to worry. But I'm not easy with it. I'm not easy with it, Jim."

She was louder now. I could imagine the basement apartment empty around her, the knot in her stomach, the mash of cigarettes in the ashtray.

"Thick as thieves, those two are. Thick as thieves. But Mike is thirteen, you know?"

"I'm sorry, I—"

"So I want you to bring him back now. I want you to go bring him back. You don't want trouble."

Her voice was cagey, but when she stopped for another drag of the cigarette her indrawn breath sounded almost like a sob.

I drove north along the highway. I had to rent a car, and its pristine smell soothed me. I told myself all would be fine, without knowing what I meant or what I was afraid I might find.

It was late September. When I reached the town closest to the lake the sun was setting. I passed the Loblaws where Lori bought her groceries that first summer. I remembered her showing off her cottage cooking, teasing my uncle, the table set in the warm screened-in porch, my mother sidelined. The ice cream stand James and I had loved was boarded up for the season, as the town prepared for winter's out-of-season poverty. The sidewalks were empty now except for a cluster of bored local teenagers on the steps of the 7-Eleven. The store glowed behind them in the dusk, their faces shadowed. I thought of James and me throwing those rocks, the blood on my shoes, his head under my hands, the water closing over his head.

I turned onto the right road, peering for names on wooden signs at the top of driveways leading down to the lake. The moon was just beginning to show through the trees.

The cottage was built near the edge of the lake, with doors

opening onto a deck, a staircase from the deck that led down to the shore. I could hear the rhythmic slapping of water on the underside of the dock. No lights were on. The place was smaller than I remembered, more rundown, the paint fading, the deck chairs turned over and pushed together, covered with a cracking blue tarp. It looked as if no one had been there for years. But James's car was in the driveway. The door was unlocked.

I stood in the hallway, where the air was damp and still. I hesitated as if trying to preserve something, some peace that hung heavy in the air. The sky had begun to cloud over: maybe it would rain.

It was so silent I almost convinced myself I'd been wrong, they couldn't be anywhere in the house. I wanted more than anything to leave James to himself, to let him go, away from me, to live some other life that had nothing to do with me. Then I heard a cough in the living room.

They were sitting across from each other in front of the fireplace like an old couple. Thick as thieves. The room was almost dark; the electricity probably hadn't been switched on. They turned to me as I came in, and they both stood up. Mike took a step forward, and I saw he lurched slightly, one leg shorter than the other.

"I told her," James said loudly, "I told her already. It's okay."

"She's very worried. It's getting late. You need to come home now."

My voice sounded unpersuasive even to me.

"Come on, Mike. I'll drive you back. James, you can take your car. I'll meet you at your place."

"No, no, no."

James waved his hands at me.

"I told her, I told her we would stay here for a while, we can stay here, it's okay."

Mike looked at me, helpless, then at James.

"Thanks, but I think I better go."

I got Mike's windbreaker from the nail by the door and handed it to him. James ran over and tugged at the sleeve of my coat.

"No, no, no, no, no—"

As I turned he bore down on me, grabbing, squawking. I hit him with my open hand. I don't know if I meant to hit him, but then I don't know how anything happens, and I did hit him, I am that man, I can't get away from it, from any of it. James was on the ground, covering his head, his glasses skittering along the floor. Mike's mouth was open like a cartoon. Neither of them moved. I bent down and took one of his hands as gently as I could.

"You're fine," I said. "Just get up."

I didn't talk to Mike on the drive back. I looked over at him from time to time, slouched into himself, licking his lips. I wondered what James wanted, what it was in this misfit boy that had caused James to make a stab at—what? I thought about James on the floor, covering his head. I knew he would pull himself together and drive home, and, as the lights of the city appeared, orange and white ahead, I knew we would never talk about what he or I had done. We would both behave as if nothing had happened, and we would go on.

He should have been a trucker: long hauls, watching the road with red-rimmed bulldog eyes, picking up boys at rest stops or gas stations, boys with soft hair and chipped uneven teeth, boys with hands curled ineptly around damp cigarettes, boys huddled beside trash cans on cold November nights. He would have been kind. Bought them food, drinks, given them money. He would have driven on through the morning with the sky blanching behind the line of trees that hide the subdivisions, the clear-cuts and garbage dumps and all that lonely space. He would have had awful breath, he would have forgotten to change his underwear, he would have worn the same shirt for three weeks, he would have had no one to take care of him. And sometimes, when the sun slanted through the windshield at first light, he would have been happy.

HOW YOU
WERE BORN

This is the story of how you were born. It's not like other stories I've told you, since you're in it. It's like nineteenth-century spirit photography where you see one person sitting in a chair and behind them something white, without features, without defined edges. Stared at long enough, the figure in the foreground fades and that trickster globule behind it takes on life, intentions, destiny.

When two women want to have a baby they immediately confront a set of obvious and insurmountable facts, and that's before there is even anyone there, before the blank-eyed creature behind the figure in the frame begins to come into focus.

The friend who will do this for us lives across the country. We asked. He said yes. That is where we are now going. I'm superstitious—it seems too easy, leaving me feeling we have pushed our luck. As we board the plane, I worry that the catch is coming.

Beside me, Molly's hand tightens on my arm. She wants this more than I can imagine wanting anything. The sunlight is weak, the pavement vast and orderly, and then the wide sky, leaving the city behind. I hate flying. For her, I have to believe we will not fall. It seems as fanciful and reckless as believing in those ghosts in old photographs.

"Are you okay?"

"Yeah."

"Really?

"Yes."

I look at my hands. We will not fall.

"Excuse me?"

The woman beside us is all white and gold, tall, whippet-thin and young. Her hair falls in complicated blonde waves, her eyebrows sleek and arched, her skin uniformly pale and smooth, dusted with powder. She wears a white wool skirt and scooped white wool top, high-heeled white boots. She reminds me of a figure on a wedding cake. Cinched and busty while also chaste and purposefully delicate, like lace or snow. It must take a lot of effort, I think, to enact a fairy-tale, a girl's overdrawn idea of an adult woman. She smiles, revealing slightly bluish teeth, pink gums.

On her lap, a little girl, three at the most, pink-cheeked, clutching a pink rabbit in one hand, kicking her feet in their pink boots.

"Can you watch her while I go to the bathroom?"

"Of course," Molly says. In every child, she tries to imagine you. The woman squeezes past us, cashmere sweater riding up as she presses by. She makes me feel worn and drab, in my jeans and old shirt, my hair unwashed, holes in my socks, as if I too, in my own way, have never become a woman. Not, like her, because I have established myself in a fantasy of girl-hood, but through simple laziness. There's something brave in her self-presentation, something gallant; I don't have the strength for it. Her daughter stares straight ahead until her mother gets back from the bathroom.

"Thanks," she says, settling back into the seat, resettling the girl on her lap. I open my book.

Alice was beginning to get very tired of sitting by her sister on the bank, and of having nothing to do: once or twice she had peeped into the book her sister was reading, but it had no pictures or conversations in it, "and what is the use of a book," thought Alice, "without pictures or conversations?"

I don't usually read children's books, but this book is part of my thesis, on sexuality and fantasy in Victorian literature. I've been working on my thesis for ten years, and nothing new emerges. Like Alice, I'm scrabbling at the leg of the glass table, never reaching the key. Still, I enjoy it, imagine writing a book of my own that will encompass the world of play and the unspoken knife-edge that all play has, the chaos at its heart. I make amused marginal notes. I'm holding Molly's hand, thinking I will read to you, my voice soft in the evenings, my life resolving miraculously around you, and you will teach me not to be afraid.

"Natalie, sit still!" The woman laughs in the half-apologetic way of someone attracting attention and glances over at me.

"She never sits still. Even for a short flight."

"Oh?"

"Never. We fly home a lot, you'd think she'd be used to it by now. Where are you going?"

I close the book.

"Stopping in Halifax."

"We're going to Truro. My brother's picking us up. Uncle Jeff. Natalie go home see uncle Jeffy?" she trills. Unexpectedly, the child wriggles away from her mother, across me and into Molly's lap.

"Oooh, sorry," the woman says. I put the book away.

"She's just so friendly, so friendly to everyone. That's us. We're people people."

She waits for me to smile.

"I'm Lola."

"Robin," I say, feeling Molly suppress a laugh. We once had a dog named Lola—a bouncing aged terrier, who barked at nothing, paws clicking, a blind blue film over its eyes.

Natalie twists round and looks Molly in the face. Very carefully, Molly puts both hands on Natalie's shoulders, touches one strand of brown hair.

"See what I mean. People people."

She strokes her own hair with one hand. Her hands will be claws someday. An emaciated well-dressed old woman, a woman with too much spare time and the petulance of someone who has no idea where the body she loved has gone. And she does love it. She arranges her skirt with an air of tangible happiness and satisfaction that's mysterious to me, as someone who's made a virtue of indifference. Her happiness might be on a timer, but she has a long way to go, still on the right side of thirty. No trace yet of that loss, that perilous arrival at irrelevance in her own eyes. She smiles at me again, guileless.

"Do you have family in Halifax?"

"No," I say. "Just friends."

I wonder where you are and who you might be and what purpose it will serve, bringing you into the world, and whether it will take or whether it will be a series of disappointments stretching on for years until, finally, we are left resigned. Molly and the little girl are staring at each other. Then Natalie claps her hands, but softly, showing Molly how to do it. They clap their hands together, *patty cake patty cake baker's man*, and Natalie laughs, a lovely screech.

"It's my granny's birthday," Lola says. "So I have to go home. Nice to get away from Toronto. Natalie's dad—my boyfriend—couldn't come. He tried but he's busy. He's a lawyer. What can you do, you know? Where do you live?"

"Oh—west, west end. Dufferin and King."

"Oh, I don't go that far west," she says. "We live on Bay Street, Natalie and me. It's really nice, with the shopping. Everything's really convenient. It's nice."

Mistress, I decide unkindly—seeing the condo, gleaming glass, white bed. Visits on the weekends, love for the secret daughter, fear that she will bore him, inability to recognize when she is boring him. The view over the city, wine glasses in the sink. She shows off the dress she has bought with his money, and he gives her a silver necklace, which he has also given to his wife, though she is too optimistic to suspect this. Tiffany's—a sales clerk greets a man who comes in every Christmas Eve and buys two identical pieces of jewellery, takes them away in identical pale blue boxes, one in each jacket pocket. She fiddles with the clasp, delighted. She's wearing it now, I can see the chain disappearing down the front of her sweater.

"But it's nice, you know? Having a break? He gets so busy. He just doesn't have time for us, sometimes."

Sweat has started under my left arm, darkening my shirt.

"I'm studying nutrition. We're going to get married when I'm done school."

Natalie has scrambled up onto her knees on Molly's lap and is leaning over the seat in front, reaching for the face of a little boy sitting between his mother and father. These people I recognize. I can place them. Big glasses sliding down the woman's nose, the man thin and lank, smiling to himself.

The tattoo on the back of his neck; her uncombed hair. They are bent toward their son, like people going home. The boy is maybe five. Natalie manages to grab a handful of his hair.

"Oh, sorry *sorry*." Lola leaps up and snatches Natalie off Molly's lap, whispering, "*Bad girl-bad-bad*." The mother in front is on her feet.

"I'm sure she didn't mean—don't worry about it, he's fine, it's nothing," she says, pulling her son up so he stands on his seat. "See, Lucas, she's just a little girl."

"Natalie, you have to say sorry."

"No, it doesn't matter—"

"Natalie, say sorry."

"Sorry." Natalie takes his indignant face in her hands and kisses him forcefully on the mouth. Lola shrieks with laughter. Now the father is also on his feet.

"Oooh, ohhh, Natalie's a funny girl. That's my funny girl. You like older men, don't you!" and no one else laughs and Lola winds down and winks at the man, who is holding the woman's hand as if he is protecting her from this strange onslaught, this creature with her helmet of gold hair.

Everyone sits down again. The woman turns around in her seat and grins at Molly and me, and the woman's grin, with her flopping hair and her uncontrived skin and the book open on her knee, is meant to be conspiratorial: we three understand each other, leaving Lola outside. We grin furtively back. Allegiance has been declared.

I don't speak to Lola again. She watches a movie on her white laptop, the glow from the screen lighting up her face. Natalie squirms unhappily in her lap.

I take Molly's hand. I open my book. I speculate about Lola's life in Toronto, now imagining her loneliness, the grey slush staining those boots as she pushes the stroller along Bay Street on a Saturday morning, the number of times a week she eats her dinner alone, a single portion pushed fretfully around her plate, her child asleep, watching the winter light fading along the city skyline. I wonder what she wanted when she started to talk to me, what she saw when she looked over at me, if she is disappointed. But you take sides. You have allegiances. You will discover that, when you are born. It's one of the first discoveries.

"We're landing." Molly says. "We're here."

The other passengers are finding their bags, tired, happy to be on the ground. I look for Lola, the white flash of her coat, the pink fuzz of Natalie's sweater, and I wave a small, half-hearted wave, and she smiles but doesn't wave back and walks off into the crowd, and as she vanishes I think of you and hope to be brave, gallant in my own way as Lola is, daring the gamble of bringing you into being.

We go out into the lobby. There he stands, shy, older than I remember, taking this very seriously, open-hearted and not knowing what to say. He puts an arm around each of us, we're lined up as if to be photographed. One, two, three, and just possibly a fourth—real and unreal as any hope, or future.

The night you were born I dreamed of a train that surged out of the dark, headlamps blazing, furious with light. It bore down on the world, shrieking, a great and terrible movement. You stared, unblinking, and your eyes were fixed on the fading afterimage of wherever we are before we are. You were more awake than anyone I had ever seen, your hands waving lightly in the new air. And I thought: this is how you were born.

ACKNOWLEDGMENTS

Thank you to Jay and Hazel Millar, for giving *How You Were Born* a new incarnation. I really don't have words.

Thank you to Malcolm Sutton, for his thoughtful editing.

Thank you to Reid Millar, Rachel Gerry, and Rachel Taylor, for your work.

Thank you to Ingrid Paulson, for designing the new cover.

Thank you to Barbara Berson, for making things happen and for her thoughtful opinions on these stories.

Early versions of some of these stories appeared in *The Antigonish Review, Event, The Fiddlehead, Prairie Fire, Plenitude,* and *The New Quarterly.* Thanks to the editors.

Thank you to Beth Follett, the publisher of the amazing and beautiful Pedlar Press, for originally championing this book, and to Beth and Alayna Munce, for editing it with such care and attention.

Thank you to friends, family, and neighbours.

Thank you to my wife Lea Ambros and our children, Livia, Tom, and Danny. For every day we've got.

PHOTO: LIVIA AMBROS

KATE CAYLEY is the author of three poetry collections, including *Lent*, a young adult novel, and two short story collections. *How You Were Born* won the Trillium Book Award and was shortlisted for the Governor General's Literary Award for Fiction. She has won an O. Henry Prize, the Mitchell Prize for Faith and Poetry, and the Geoffrey Bilson Award for Historical Fiction for Young People. She has been a finalist for the K. M. Hunter Award, the Carter V. Cooper Short Story Prize, and the Firecracker Award for Fiction, and longlisted for the Frank O'Connor International Short Story Award and the CBC Literary Prizes in both poetry and fiction. Cayley's plays have been produced in Canada, the US, and the UK, and she is a frequent collaborator with immersive company Zuppa Theatre. Cayley lives in Toronto with her wife and their three children.

COLOPHON

Manufactured as the tenth-anniversary edition of
How You Were Born
in the spring of 2024 by Book*hug Press

Edited for the press by Malcolm Sutton
Copy edited by Rachel Taylor
Proofread by Laurie Siblock
Type + design by Ingrid Paulson
Cover image: ©iStockPhoto/CSA Printstock
Printed in Canada

bookhugpress.ca